I used to be

I used to be

Mary Brown

First Published 2017 by Fantastic Books Publishing

Cover design by Gabi

ISBN (eBook): 9781912053520
ISBN (paperback): 9781912053537

To Molly Tandy, my lovely mother and a wonderful grandmother to my children.

I used to be

I shouldn't be here.

'Where am I?' My voice sounds thin, owl-like, an old woman's voice not much used.

I shouldn't be anywhere.

'In hospital, dear.' The voice smiles.

It looks like a hospital. Beds, each with its drip attached: miniature water-towers like those that used to feed the thirsty steam trains of my childhood.

* * *

I remember the remains of a water-tower on the Tip. It had lost its life-giving tube, unlike the water-towers here, and looked a bit like a gallows: a symbol of death in that place of life. So incongruous. The Tip: that triangular piece of wasteland, seen from any train approaching any large railway station. On two sides the lines diverged as they made their ways to different sides of the country, carrying the connected to their connections. On our Tip, the third, shorter side was bounded by a decaying terrace of Victorian houses, some boarded up, awaiting demolition, some housing a few of society's rejects. The girls no longer watched the trains, just as those who raced past, thinking they knew where they were going, lost in their laptops, did not see the no-man's-island Tip, or appreciate its anarchic yellow ragwort. Sometimes trains stopped for a while outside the station, and we could see the empty faces of passengers, like people in a queue, exasperated. When someone waved to us, the girls would make rude gestures back, later they ignored them, stopped being interested in the silent quarrels, kisses, children's screams or other dramas behind the double glazed windows. The Krew had long ago ceased to bother that someone might see them, that they might be in trouble for trespassing on the Tip. It was their Tip now, their Shack. There they were safe from the real world, or perhaps this was their reality, their escape. I needed that too, needed them. Away across the lines, beyond the rusting gasometer, was the hospital, with its dire warning, looming above its surroundings: where I am now?

The girls did not see beyond their Tip, where, among piles of ancient rubbish, buddleia bushes struggled, pale violet rather than the flamboyant purple of suburban gardens. Here and there a pathetic echo of a tree, possibly a silver birch, defied the coal dark soil, which seemed to grow nothing else but straggling thistles, nettles and the ubiquitous ragwort.

I saw the Tip as a kind of island. Like all islands it was approached through treacherous waters, yet it kept its islanders safe. Like all islands, it had its Caliban, its noises. Kayleigh's Krew brought to this scar from an industrial past, their present troubles, their scarred lives, and somehow found strength to cope with the terrifying realities of the world beyond. The girls of the Krew would sit on upturned milk crates, those old style metal ones, and share their miseries and frustrations. I was never sure why they allowed me to come and feed the cats, and listen, but at the time it seemed natural.

The Tip and Kayleigh's Krew gave me back my life, just as it helped the Krew to cope with theirs. There we could just be. Now I've chosen not to be, but it seems this isn't allowed. How did I get here?

* * *

'Why am I in hospital?'

The smiling voice has gone.

I shouldn't be here.

I haven't been in a hospital, apart from those tests, since the day Mark was born.

* * *

How well I remember that day. I hadn't expected it to be easy, Kayleigh was not an easy child, why should she be any different giving birth? An epidural was prescribed early, but this didn't stop her histrionic screams, learned, I suspected, from television. In other circumstances, perhaps, Kayleigh might have had a stage career.

I remember the midwife's exasperated, 'Push, dear, push. You must help your little one into the world.'

Kayleigh ignored her, pushing ineffectually between what must have been disturbing, even if painless, contractions.

'Push when I tell you, dear.'

'I'll push when I fucking wants. Whose baby is this?'

'You need to push with the contractions, you know that.'

'Remember your breathing,' I said, trying to sooth a writhing Kayleigh, cursing myself for encouraging her wish to be the mother of this child born of despair, out of a whim.

'Fuck off! I want to stop breathing. I just want to be dead.' Another scream.

'Think of baby.'

'Fuck the baby. And you. Go away and let me die.'

The midwife, working hard to ignore Kayleigh's swearing, finally said, 'Kayleigh, Kayleigh, that's enough ...'

'Yeah. And I've had enough of you, and all.'

'You're upsetting the other mothers.'

'And you're upsetting me, Paki. Fuck the other mothers, they must be as fucking crazy as I was. Who wants to be a mother? I'll have her took into care!'

She did not hear me say, quietly, not sure if it was true, 'You don't mean that.'

'You'd think no one had ever had a baby before. Your mum went through all this for you,' the midwife's infinite patience was almost exhausted.

'More fool her, then. I never asked to be born, any more than this poor little sod did.'

4

The midwife now ignored her, concentrating on sucking the child safely into the world with a ventouse cup. Finally she put the tiny yellowish grey baby, covered in slime, screaming on Kayleigh's chest.

'A lovely little boy, with a good pair of lungs.'

Kayleigh stopped crying instantly: the midwife's relief lasted only moments.

'There's been a mistake, my baby's a girl.' She pushed him away, crossed her arms against him.

'Your mistake, I'm afraid, my dear, there's no mistaking his sex.'

'I'm not your fucking dear. I ain't been carrying a boy around all this time.'

'Who said it was a girl?'

'I just knowed it were. I don't want no fucking boy.'

Exhausted by the long hours of emotion, I almost shouted, 'He's a baby, Kayleigh, your baby! A boy baby.'

* * *

Now it seems I am the one in hospital. I hope I'm not behaving quite like Kayleigh did, but it is so frustrating. I am so thirsty. There is a jug of water. And a glass. But I don't seem able to sit up and get it. I am so tired. And thirsty.

* * *

I remember how once Kayleigh used to scare me slightly, I'm not sure why. Her strident giggle somehow got into my stomach, stirred up my digestion, like fleas inside me. Boys don't giggle, though sometimes mine would guffaw at jokes that to me were incomprehensible. The giggles of Kayleigh's Krew wafted across the Tip. A substitute for tears. Kayleigh's giggles seemed worse than the others'.

Kayleigh said she was an accidental child, claiming her mother conceived her after a quickly forgotten accident, her birth an accident, her existence not noticed until it was too late to 'do something' about it. 'Soon as I saw you, I just loved you to bits,' her mother was fond of saying, and Kayleigh of repeating. It seemed to me that only on the Tip could she hold these bits together. Despite maternal indifference, she survived the accidents of childhood. Now, when I tried to offer her a way out, as she repeated her mother's accident, it seemed to have been a terrible mistake.

'He's lovely. Look at his long hair, his tiny fingers.' I hadn't remembered how small new born babies were, how vulnerable; his minute face was wrinkled, like an old oak apple.

Kayleigh was not looking, she exploded, 'He's disgusting. All fucking slimy. Can't they be bothered to wash him?'

'They will,' I said, remembering the little sanitised blue bundles I'd been handed, long after I'd cried out, 'I want to hold him.'

'He's been inside you so long,' I said now, 'he needs to get used to being outside. Look, he's stretching out his little hand, feeling for you.'

Kayleigh looked for a moment, could her disgust be melting, perhaps only temporarily? But her glance had no welcome for her son, his fingers were boys' fingers.

'Take him away and clean him up,' she ordered, 'and don't bring him back.'

Baby was taken away.

As the six-and-a-half pounds of humanity struggled to be a part of the world, Kayleigh, exhausted by her struggles, fell into a deep sleep, or was she pretending? I stayed with her, as she was put to bed in a single room. Eventually the tiny blue blanketed baby, only his face showing beneath a little knitted cap, was placed in the cot beside her.

The absolute helplessness of the new baby, touched me deeply. So fragile, so dependent: its new life so easily extinguishable. The only person not touched by this child seemed to be his mother, who pushed him away when she was woken by his thin cry, and a nurse trying to put him into her arms.

'Fuck off! Go to hell!' Kayleigh turned over, groaned, and went back to sleep.

I couldn't believe it. After all I'd done for her, all we'd all done. All the lies I'd told, the crimes I'd committed. All for nothing ...?

* * *

I wonder if I've got the strength to sit up? I would really like a sip of that water. It sits there, tempting me, almost a rainbow on the top of the glass. Rainbow. I knew Kay was special, exceptional, from that day of the rainbow.

* * *

I remember I had been sheltering in the Shack from a torrential downpour when she suddenly appeared, sodden, her hair hanging down like seaweed, her out-grown school sweatshirt clinging to her thin body revealing a surprisingly adult form. She was radiant in her wetness, her eyes shone, not just with her defiant rebelliousness. She needed to talk to someone; I was the only one around just then. I could feel her looking at me, and got the distinct impression that she would have preferred one of her Krew. She made do with me.

'Orlright,' she said. This was the Krew's usual greeting, but I was never sure if it was a question or a statement. Nor what the correct reply was. Orlright, I think, but I never managed to say it.

'I'm all right, Kayleigh, how are you?'

'Fuck it, Maude, d'you see that rainbow?'

I looked up. I hadn't seen a rainbow for years, this one seemed special; the sky was an incredible colour.

'Catch you up,' Kayleigh told me she had said to the others at the supermarket, where she and a few of the Krew spent their lunch hours; but school seemed even more irrelevant than usual, so she did not follow them, not even to get her mark. When she reached the Tip, she had hoped that, secretly alone, a strange disturbing feeling she had might go away. Now it was fading, and she was slightly sorry. Only slightly. She was not used to feelings, she told me. She had flopped carelessly down on the harsh ground, gazing up at the blue above.

'I felt well weird, Maude,' she told me.

I think she was in that liminal place where one state merges into another, on the boundary between sleep and wakefulness, moving between childhood and adolescence, somewhere between contentment and panic, between dreams and reality, happiness and misery, where things become but never are, where we cannot stay. This is holy ground.

She said she wondered how the sky could be so blue. She didn't usually think about the sky, it was just up there, no more remarkable than the pavement down here, both grey. She lay among the gloriously poisonous ragwort, under the blue, with its invitation to we were neither of us sure what, feeling strangely at peace. It was one of those rare days when even happiness seemed possible. As the sun warmed that vulnerable gap between her grimy school sweatshirt, which suddenly seemed much too tight, and that shapeless grey skirt, worn carefully half an inch shorter than regulation, she luxuriated in, without understanding, this unaccustomed sensation of contentment.

'I could feel me heart beating, pumping me blood round me body,' she had said. 'In a strange way, slightly scary, I feel me body's no longer mine. I'd always said to Mum, "It's me fucking body, innit, I'll eat what I fucking wants. It's me hair, I'll have it whatever colour I chooses".'

Now her body was changing without her permission. 'Right weird,' she said.

She said she had looked up at the smiling ragwort flowers, whose faces echoed the sun, yellow and round. That was how she used to paint the sun in infant school: her pictures were always green at the bottom, blue at the top, white clouds, a satisfying yellowy-orange blob of a sun, with lines streaming out on all sides like ragwort petals. Sometimes a house or a lonely person in the middle; usually the middle was empty, there was never time for it after the top and the bottom. Now there was this strange feeling of peacefulness: nothing mattered, apart from the light and the heat, she seemed part of the peace around her.

I think Kayleigh was fully in the present. The future could be ignored, the past forgotten. If you'd asked her then how she felt, she'd have said, 'Fucking weird.'

So she shut her eyes, let go, slipping over the boundary, wrapped in the forgiving forgetfulness of the blue, drifting peacefully, dreamlessly, into a sleep quite unlike that of her nightly escape in bed.

Nothing could last. Suddenly the blue gave way, without

warning, to dark grey, the warmth to cold. The sun was replaced by a menacing cloud, somewhere between black and purple, shutting out the light; it felt darker after the blinding sun, colder after the heat. Startled by the transformation, she found herself, again without warning, wet: her nostrils filled with the delicate scent of rain on hot, dry soil, with its faint promise that the world will never end in drought. Kayleigh noticed 'that weird smell', but did not recognise it; she was so wet, so quickly, she had no time to think. Slowly picking herself up, she ran slowly to the Shack.

'By the time I got here I were soaked.' Shivering, because although not cold, she was much colder, she looked out at the transformed Tip, deafened by the storm on the corrugated iron. The Shack sheltered us both. That remains of an ancient building, in distinctive railway redbrick, some greying bricks suggesting it was once painted white, blackened with soot from long gone steam trains, the letters G.W.R. just visible to those old enough to remember the old Great Western Railway, before nationalisation. It was almost the only building from the steam age to remain standing on the Tip. The past existence of others was marked by a few patches of concrete half hidden in the struggling grass. The Shack, with its three crumbling walls, few slates on what was left of its roof, which the girls had struggled to repair with sheets of rusty corrugated iron, was no protection against today's rain.

A silence hung between us: we looked across the Tip. The sun was still shining somewhere beyond the railway; we watched the rainbow together in amazement. The colours grew brighter, each drizzling into the next, so that you couldn't be certain what colour was what, like the reds and yellows of a sunset. It was clear, far clearer than your average rainbow, yet still hazy …

Kayleigh told me that she remembered something about rainbows: what was it? Something in science? No? Was there a rainbow in the Bible? Did Jesus walk on a rainbow? As she explored her memory, at the same time wondering why she was bothering, a second rainbow appeared outside the first. A double rainbow. I'm not sure I'd ever seen such a thing before, they fitted together perfectly: made for each other. Beautiful. Holy. Then Kayleigh remembered: God sent a rainbow as some sort of a sign. Of what?

Then she remembered the science bit.

'We looked through triangles of solid glass to see rainbows, something to do with light mixing up the colours. Old Ratty let a few of us at a time look through the glasses, worried that someone might drop or nick them.' That science lesson came back to her as we watched the rainbow slowly fade.

The rainbows they'd seen through the glass had been tiny, but mind-blowing, appearing where light met darkness.

'Look! Old Ratty's got a rainbow round his head,' she had said to Suze.

'Everyone was wearing rainbows, like halos in church windows, but brighter.'

They were captivated, forgot this was school, where everything's boring. Together they took turns with the glass, going to the window looking outside. The great tree in the playground, huge, green, comforting in a strange way. Looking through the glass, the tree was covered with hundreds, thousands, of tiny, brilliant rainbows where the sun met dark leaves.

They were in another world of beauty and wonder. But this was school, it couldn't last.

'Ratty said, "Kayleigh! You deaf or something? Bring the prism back. Now!"'

Prism. That's what the glass thing was called. Prism. Prison. Just one letter different, and everything changed.

I thought of the delight of the secret world of the prism, and the ordered reality of school: a prison, where teachers destroyed any chance of freedom. I wondered if she felt yet another door was closing around her?

We stared now at the familiar scene, magically transformed, almost unrecognisable. The view was extraordinary: the fading rainbow, once more single, the yellow ragwort, purple cloud, sun shining beyond the silver railway lines, the noise of trains drowned by the rain battering the corrugated iron, and that weird, tantalising smell. The towering hospital chimney shone across the railway to the collapsing water-tower. Kayleigh said she felt part of it all, perhaps because so much of the rain was in her clothes, her hair, her eyes. I wondered then if the Tip had some secret magic.

Then, as suddenly as it started, the rain stopped. The purple cloud passed over and the sun reappeared. We went outside and basked in it: Kayleigh was soon dry. The sound of the trains replaced the thumping of the outsize raindrops ...

I remember The Tip was the last place I'd gone in search of Tiddly. I'd seen it many times in the past, but never looked at it. Now it appeared the sort of place a lost cat might hide. You could only get there through the garden of the end house, where sometimes homeless people moved in, but didn't stay. I saw the gap in the fence, but was scared of the youths lounging in the garden, apparently half asleep: what could the other half be?

Summoning up my courage, I braved the garden, carefully avoiding the patches of vomit. In hot weather these were caked dry by the sun, the surface cracked like gravy on a plate the washing up forgot; after rain, they were half washed away, spread over the path, waiting for a passing seagull or slug to gobble them up. I had to step over the indestructible containers of hastily consumed suppers which blew around the garden and the Tip, among the broken glass, half decayed magazines, their colours fading, and, sometimes, discarded syringes. All this joined the clinging mingled scents of tom cat and rotting vegetation, suggesting why the Krew called it the Tip. The name reminded me of a parent's description of a teenage bedroom, although I doubt if any of these girls' mothers bothered about the state of their bedrooms, if they had bedrooms.

I squeezed through the gap in the rusty spiked railings, and set off calling, 'Puss, puss, puss,' more and more loudly. The youths took no notice of me; I didn't dare ask them if they'd seen Tiddly. As I slowly, painfully crossed the wasteland, I saw the Shack, and the collection of girls, who must have been playing truant from school, as I was from life. They were dressed in what was once school uniform, but their pathetic attempts to make themselves more alluring, made them look slightly ridiculous. I didn't know then that this was their space, or understand why I felt an immediate kinship with them. Did they recognise me as another outcast? Like them, so hurt, so bruised, by life. Hurt by people, by society, motorbikes, husbands, parents, teachers, schools. I shut myself away; they banded together. And yet they let me join them. Why? Was it because we lived in the same limbo, and somehow they must have recognised this?

'Have you seen a cat?'

The girls shook their heads, joined in, in a desultory way, calling, 'Puss, puss, puss.' Eventually a starved looking black cat appeared, obviously expecting something, and rubbed itself against me. My heart rose with the familiar warm scent of damp fur. I bent down and stroked it; it purred, its fur slightly rough, not at all like Tiddly's sleekness. It was hungry.

'I'll bring you some food tomorrow.'

'Take it home with you, why don't you?' said one of the girls.

'No, I think he belongs here.' I wondered why I said that, surely what I needed was another cat.

'I'm a bit scared of those men in the garden, is there another way out?'

'They're smack heads,' said another girl, 'well out of it.'

'Out of their fucking heads innit,' said another. 'They won't notice you. Know what I means.'

'Thanks,' I said, unsure what I was thanking them for.

As I walked away I heard them discussing me, their languid voices and their giggles carrying over the waste ground.

'What you want to encourage the old bag for, Kayles?'

'She do stink. Her face looks like a cow-pat that's been rained on, but she's harmless.'

Did I stink? I tried to remember when I'd last had a bath.

'I think she's some kind of a witch,' said the girl I later knew as Suzy, 'desperate for a black cat; all that long, greasy, grey hair. She's got hairs sprouting on her chin.' They giggled. Suzy was between childhood's witches, confined to story books, and the all too real adult ones. The kids in the street, long ago, used to call, 'Hey witch,' when I went out to the shops. Do witches have hair on their chins?

Did I recognise myself from their descriptions? I knew I looked like a walking Oxfam shop. A witch would have looked better.

'She's fucking batty, but harmless,' Kayleigh said.

'Let her come.'

'We can't fucking stop her, can we?'

'We could if we really wanted.'

Could they hear the silent wailing of my misery? For years I hadn't really minded what others thought of me. Was this the beginning of a new life? How much did I hear, and how much did I think I'd heard?

'What do we want with cats, Kayles?'

'They're harmless and all, Shel. Won't do us no harm. Probably won't see her again, anyway.'

But they did. They were there the next day, and the next. I continued to visit the Tip, to feed the cat, learning how the girls lived on the fringe of society, a different fringe from mine, yet similar enough for me to feel their hurt. Did they feel mine? Gradually I became more than tolerated; some kind of rapport with the Krew began to form, and to sustain me. It still mystifies me, as I am sure it mystified them, if they ever experienced mystification. Did they realise the common bond of those on the margins, the marginalised? We who seem to have no place in the great scheme of things, if there is such a thing. Looking back, I was sure there was an invisible, intangible thread linking us, some feeling of commonality. It was my lost cat that brought me to their space, but they had no time for cats, that was not the bond. But they, and I, were as lost as Tiddly. We belonged together. Had Kayleigh recognised that when she labelled me 'harmless'? A new label for me; I hoped to live up to it. I think I eventually did better than that.

Coming to the Tip to feed that cat, and others that appeared from time to time, became part of my life, almost a reason for continuing to live, as, until then, grief at the loss of Michael, and the shame of being divorced had kept me alive. The Krew, like me, seemed neither part of the real world, nor able to escape it. Their reality was here on the Tip. Increasingly it became mine. I think we communicated mostly in silence, which is not the contradiction it might at first seem.

I soon learned their spoken language, which at first seemed like a foreign tongue. As they immersed me in it, I got the sense of what they were saying, even if I didn't understand all their words …

I remember my long years of mourning. Grief moved in when Michael died, and had been my constant companion ever since, casting his grey shadow over my entire existence. He cut me off from other people, denied me joy. Even food had less taste, oranges were less orange, bananas had the texture of potatoes, the scents of flowers were filtered, semi-skimmed, all was diminished. Grief replaced Worry in my life. Grief became an elderly cat, comforting, sleeping at night on the foot of my bed, or an all-enveloping grey shawl.

'You are in my power,' growled Grief, and I humbly, gratefully accepted him. He protected me from life. He showed me that it was my duty to Michael to live in misery. I fell deeper and deeper into that black hole. Grief held my hand, fell with me. I existed in a semi-human state and wished for no more …

Women experience grief differently from men; as they do most things differently, but with grief the difference is more destructive. Husband and I reacted each in our own way to Michael's death. I remembered his birth, and wept. I remembered his first steps, and wept. I saw him start school, move on to grammar school, leave, get his first job, his only job, and I railed at the waste of all that careful preparation – for what? For death. It was obscene. I screamed, rejected Husband's attempts at comfort, rejected his very different grief. While I wept and screamed and remembered, he silently buried his memories, they were too painful, he could not accept them.

I wailed at the waste, the if-only's, the might-have-beens. Husband kept all these, and his hurt, hidden within. I was open, not caring who knew of my misery: his grief was secret, silent. To him I was making a spectacle of myself, with my ostentatious display. To me he was uncaring. I screamed at his lack of concern. Locked in our separate griefs for a common loss, we suffered together, separately, neither accepting the other's sorrow. Husband tried to put it all behind him. Had he? Could he? I could not. Had not.

* * *

'Why am I in hospital?'

The smiling voice has gone.

I look at my water-tower, securely strapped to the back of my hand and lie for what seems like a long time, savouring the peace I somehow feel in the midst of the hospital turmoil. Like the peace we found on the Tip, between the noisy trains … I really would like a sip of that water.

I shouldn't be here.

'How did I get here?'

The voice has returned to inject my water-tower.

'In an ambulance, dear.'

I've never been in an ambulance … Did it flash its lights, ring its bell? Ambulances don't have bells nowadays, they have those dreadful sirens, whose agonised cries ring out across the Tip as they ferry their victims, echoing the banshee wails of the manic seagulls. Over the railway lines, over the docks, over elegant regency squares and squalid Victorian side streets the gulls fly, then off to the municipal tip on the other side of the city in search of food. Their cries taunt the patients in the high hospital wards, and those locked in the prison below, with their savage cries of freedom … I didn't hear the ambulance dragging me back to life.

'How did I get to the ambulance?'

'You're a very lucky girl. Some ramblers found you. Or rather their dog did. You thank your lucky stars for that dog. Now try and get some rest.' She hurries away.

I never did like dogs. Nasty, dirty disturbers of the peace. Spoiling country walks, attacking cats, frightening away wildlife. So it was a dog that robbed me of my peace. I might have guessed.

'Dogs! Dogs!'

'Hush, dear, there are no dogs here. Try and rest.' She almost touches me. I turn away.

I don't mind confessing, I'm scared of dogs. They sense this and snarl at me. The owner looks hurt, and always says, 'He won't hurt you,' (it's always the he's that snarl) in that voice kept for those who don't like dogs. I don't trust them. Their wolf inheritance is not that deeply hidden. They pander to man's lowest instincts: territory, brute force, the love of slavish devotion. That dog will probably become a local tabloid hero.

I was in that place of perfect peace. Did I hear it shattered by barking? I only remember the peace. Even as I remember it, it's slipping away. I begin to feel indignant. I realise that the peace, drifting slowly, so slowly, away is the absolute, perfect peace that can only come through death. It has eluded me. Somehow I have been dragged back to life, but I'm too weak to express my indignation …

* * *

I remember the boys wanted a dog. Begged, pestered Husband and me for years, but eventually they learned to love cats. Cats are different. If it hadn't been for cats I'd never have met Kayleigh and her Krew …

I remember that dreadful day, all those years ago, perhaps only five, but it feels like another lifetime, when I finally had to accept that Tiddly was no more. Tiddly had disappeared a few days before, and when he went I realised that in all the years I'd lived alone, I'd never been alone. Now, with Tiddly's defection, I sensed true loneliness for the first time. Tiddly: the last remaining cat of a family that numbered seven at its height – some strays the boys found, whom we'd been unable to reunite with their owners, some offspring of inadvertently un-neutered members of the family. Tiddly was special. He was the son of Benjy, a misdiagnosed female, who herself was the daughter of darling Nibbly, whom we'd acquired when the boys were small: third generation cat. I had buried the cats, one by one, in the back garden, where once Granddad grew his prize-winning vegetables, which Husband's could never match. Now the garden was all rank grass, the soil so hard that each grave was more of an effort to dig. I couldn't even perform this final service for Tiddly.

I hadn't touched another human being for years, yet took for granted the feel of a cat's fur beneath my hand as I stroked him. Every evening the cat flap would rattle as Tiddly came in, damp from his crepuscular adventures, and jumped on to my lap as I sat by the gas fire, its familiar hiss joining our conversation. Every evening for years I stroked and he purred; half purring myself, half singing – a strange shared language understood by us both. Then, for no apparent reason, he would jump up and depart, the cat flap rattling once more. Then I would turn out the fire, fill a hot water bottle and drag myself up the narrow stairs, taking care not to trip on the greasy hole in the carpet, sink into my unmade bed, pull the blankets around me, and drift into dreamless oblivion.

Then Tiddly stopped going out, spending his nights instead on my bed. In the last few days he'd found the cat flap too heavy for him, and started to mess in the kitchen, once in the bedroom. I thought of taking him to a vet, but, though my conscious mind refused to contemplate the possibility, I knew deep down that there was nothing to be done. He was eating less and less, snoring more and more loudly, venturing out hardly at all. Tiddly would soon be joining Michael.

Why did I continue to search for Tiddly? I knew he must be dead. What hopeless hope was it that made me cry plaintively, 'Puss, puss, puss'? For years now all my conversation had been with him. How could he desert me? How could I continue to live without him? It must have been some deep urge to live that drew me out of the house that wet morning. The previous evening he'd cried at the cat flap and I'd opened the door. He paused on the step, feeling the air, cool after the heat of the fire, and then ventured gingerly over the threshold into the night. I watched him, thinking perhaps he was getting better, wanting to be out this evening.

I woke expecting to feel him on the bed, and when he wasn't, I started to panic, my cries of 'Puss, puss, puss,' becoming increasingly desperate, disturbing the morning silence. I moved furniture that had not been moved for years, layers of dust rose to rebuke me. I searched every unlikely corner of the house, my cries of 'Puss, puss, puss,' turning to sobs. I forgot to make my tea and, as the darkness retreated, went out and called 'Puss, puss, puss' to the careless dawn …

I remember that day when Kayleigh told me she was pregnant, after the night of the great storm, when we were together on the Tip. She was Kayleigh then, became Kay only gradually. I felt privileged that she told me before the others in the Krew. The wind had been growing more violent all night, but that wasn't what kept me awake. I'd spent much of the night in thought, unaware of the storm. I was realising why I continued to come to the Tip: the girls gave me strength, and, through them, I felt on the verge of re-connecting with my fellow human beings. But I am an adult, it should be for me to support the girls, not to cling to their life support network, like a black fly on a broad bean. I'd been startled the previous day, when they asked me for advice. I'd failed them and myself. I should have been able to answer their question. I wished I could help these girls, but couldn't then see how.

That day I saw Kayleigh alone by the Shack and was almost glad to see her. She looked decidedly unwell. I was not sure if she'd seen me, she wasn't looking in my direction, and the noise of a passing train made it useless to call out. The Shack shook, as it frequently did when an express went by. When its noise died it was replaced by a sudden crescendo of the rushing wind. It shook the Shack; first with gentle almost playful little bouts, stirring up the dust, then subsiding. Soon the attack became stronger, more threatening. The cardboard nailed over broken windows was blown inwards, letting in the storm. The pauses between gusts grew shorter, the wind became continuous, with occasional even more powerful bursts. One of these removed a sheet of corrugated iron from the roof. The noise was fearful; I followed Kayleigh into the Shack, as the other two sheets landed with sickening shrieks, worse than the howling wolf wind. For a time neither of us spoke, we almost huddled up together against the uncontrollable gale, which subsided as quickly as it had grown, leaving just a normal windy day, blowing the rubbish around, bending the ragwort, hustling cool air into the Shack.

It must be the equinox, that time when the darkness starts to outlast the light. The wind blows strongest when the year is on the turn, each day darker than the last. Why should this provoke such clamour in the air? The wind rattles windows, whistles up chimneys, devastates the best tended gardens: runner beans flattened, sunflowers blown sideways, leaves carpeting the tidiest lawns. This battle between dark and light is even worse at the spring equinox, when light wins the contest, and blows away the winter.

This wind was desperate; in the spring it is more refreshing, rejuvenating. Light and darkness each refuse to yield without a struggle; the balance of the year seems to bring imbalance with it. I knew that when the wind died away, if I bothered to look, I'd find most trees had lost their leaves, resumed their winter shapes, revealed their inner structure. Others, more tenacious, would hold on to autumn, only reluctantly releasing their leaves one by one into the once more still air. The wind made conversation impossible. In the noisy silence a picture appeared in my mind of the Severn Bore. I remembered that day, years ago when Granddad took Gran and me to see that equinoctial tidal wave. Young though I was, I had been aware of witnessing something special, holy even, and fallen silent in awe of the bore, and its testimony to human powerlessness in the face of nature.

I'd never quite experienced that sensation again, until, perhaps, that day on the Moor – was it yesterday? Strangely, on that far away day by the river, the silence was also broken by a hysterical dog, who was charging down the river bank, invading our peace. The spell was broken. The crowd that had gathered to watch in silence started to talk, and to make their ways home.

I returned unwillingly to the present, 'Are you all right, Kayleigh?' The wind dropped slightly.

Kayleigh turned, and looked at me, distress pouring from her, like flood water. She looked both fit and ill at the same time. She didn't reply at first, then slowly, 'Yeah … Nah … yeah, I'm fine. Nah … I'm fucking pregnant.'

'Are you sure?'

'I done a test.'

'Oh dear. Have you told your parents?'

'Fuck it, Mau, I couldn't do that.'

'Why not?'

'Mum'd kill me. Me so-called step-dad'd probably make me kill the baby. Then he'd kill me. They'd shout at me. Blame me. Then they'd blame each other. Then they'd go for me again. You don't know me mum, Mau, she's not like the mums you sees on the telly ads. I can't talk to her like. Can't tell her something like that. I can't. I fucking can't. They'd both go bananas, Mau, know what I means?'

Kayleigh started to cry. I was embarrassed. I wanted to put an arm around her, kiss her, tell her she'd be all right, Auntie Maude would take care of everything. But I couldn't. Kayleigh was sitting on a milk crate, I was hovering above her, leaning down uncomfortably. I would have to pull another crate over to get near enough to hug her, which wouldn't be very spontaneous. After a pause, however, I did that, feeling awkward: it was so very long since I had put an arm round anyone, I seemed to have forgotten how arms worked. But once started, I found the long unused movements had been asleep inside me all those years, and they creaked back to life. To my surprise, Kayleigh hugged me back, and cried louder. I let her cry, still holding her, although the crate was not near enough and my arm and back started to ache, but I didn't dare to move. After what seemed like a long time Kayleigh's sobs decreased, she pulled away from me.

We sat in silence for a time then I said, 'Have you thought what are you going to do, Kayleigh?'

'Have a kid.'

Silence. Then I said, 'There is an alternative, you know.'

Kayleigh jumped back as if I'd head-butted her. 'You means I could fucking kill it? Have it killed? Do it in? Poor little thing, it's got a right to live hasn't it? Why do people always think it's OK to kill them before they're born, but afterwards … you wouldn't tell me to kill it after it were born, would you?'

'It's not the same.'

'Isn't it? Why not? It's a fucking baby innit?'

'It's a foetus.'

'I can't kill it, Mau. It's come to me for a bit of love. I'll have someone to love, to care for like. I might teach me fucking mum. I wants this baby. Me mum didn't want me, or she wouldn't treat me like she does. I'll show her.'

'I thought you weren't going to tell your mum.'

'I'll show her how to love a kid, once I've got it. I'll love it like no kid's ever been loved, know what I means? And it'll love me, right.'

'Kayleigh, it's not that easy. Where will you live, if your mum won't have you?'

'They'd give me a house, or a flat, if I had a kid. I've seen it on telly. If you're pregnant they gives you a council flat, right.'

'Is that why you did it?'

'No!' Kayleigh was angry with me now. 'If I'd done that I'd have realised I were carrying months ago.'

'When is it due?'

'Dunno.'

'When did you notice you'd not been having your periods?'

'I didn't. I just realised yesterday. Wanting fucking chocolate so bad. Pregnant craving, like.'

She told me that the previous day, when Tiger had lit a cigarette, and offered her one, she had shaken her head. Then wondered why she'd refused. She realised she hadn't smoked for a few weeks: had she given up? Right now what she had needed was some chocolate. Could one need chocolate the way one needed cigarettes? She'd taken two bars from the newsagents, intending to share them, but had eaten them both on the way. That was wrong, needing chocolate that bad. She remembered Mum saying she was getting fat, she must be really fat for Mum to notice. She hadn't nicked sweets much since leaving junior school. But now she felt a real craving for chocolate. A craving? Craving! And putting on weight? She'd felt herself going white, then ran off away from the others. She knew why she couldn't run as fast as she wanted.

I tried not to smile when Kayleigh told me how she'd realised she was pregnant, 'When was your last period, then?' I tried again.

'Dunno. I don't take much fucking notice generally. It's been a while now, I think. Dunno.'

'When was the last time you … you … went with a boy?' I searched uneasily for the right words.

'Had sex you mean? When did I last have a fuck, right? I ain't had sex, not that way. Don't like men. It were just the once. It were right awful. I don't want to talk about it. I thought I'd put it out of me head. It didn't occur to me it could give me a kid. Not the once, know what I means? Not when you didn't want it. It were a right mess. I'm not talking about it, right.'

'No, no you needn't. Can you remember when this was? Then we can work out when the baby will come.'

'It'll come when it's fucking ready. Don't make much difference when. Must have been a few months ago now. It were a hot day. I weren't wearing that much. I don't want to talk about it, know what I mean.'

'They'll do a scan at the hospital. They can see how big the baby is and when it will be born.'

'I'm not going to no hospital. I'm fucking not. Right.'

'Kayleigh, if you want to have the baby, if you want to love it, you must give it a good start in life. You must get medical help.'

'I'm only fourteen, right. I heard on the telly like they said like it were much safer to have a baby when you was young like. We was meant to have kids in our teens, innit. I won't need no doctors, no hospitals. I'll be OK. I will.'

I said nothing. If Kayleigh was to have a baby, and have it safely, she needed to see a doctor soon. And she had to tell her parents. Had she wanted an abortion, I thought it might be possible without her parents knowing, but having a baby must be different. I looked at Kayleigh and realised that she looked pregnant. Although she'd put on little weight, her hair shone, her face looked clear, eyes bright. Behind her distress she looked brimming with health, as I had done in my own pregnancies. Perhaps there was no great hurry. Kayleigh could go on a bit longer thinking she could get a council flat and have a baby without telling her parents.

We sat in silence for a while; I felt uncomfortable.

A few of the girls of the Krew were wandering leisurely across the Tip. When they were within earshot, Kayleigh called to them, 'Guess what? I'm fucking preg!'

'No!' said Suze. She could not know that her mother would have been delighted to hear this news; proof to her that her daughter's unsuitable friendship was at least not with a lesbian.

'Yeah. Up the duff. Expecting.'

In the silence that followed, I wondered again at the girls' capacity for saying nothing, and it feeling completely natural. Silences and giggles seemed to complement each other.

There were no giggles today. I had always felt that silences should be filled, but I couldn't fill this one. Eventually Suze said quietly, 'What are you going to do, Kayles?'

'Fuck knows. I'm going to have a baby, right.' She looked defiantly round, daring them to contradict her.

'You could get rid of it, know what I means,' said Shellie.

'Why should I want to kill me fucking baby, Shel?'

'I dunno. You're only fourteen, Kayles, innit. You don't want to be a mum does you?'

'Who says I don't?'

'Does you?'

'Yeah, well. I thinks I does and all. Know what I means?'

There was another silence. Then the girls made a succession of suggestions, all of which she rejected, until Shellie said, 'Well, you could come and live here, on the Tip.'

At first all the girls rejected the idea. Shellie's suggestions were generally rejected, but after a while Kayleigh said, 'I dunno. Perhaps you've got a point for once.'

I was relieved when Suzy poured scorn on the idea, but the other girls took it seriously. They would repair the Shack's leaking roof, find furniture and carpets on skips, light a fire and burn the coal that lay all over the Tip. Sam would steal camping equipment from her foster parents.

Should I intervene or let them have their dream; it was harmless, wasn't it? But there would have to be a sensible plan sometime. Why not now? What could they do? Go to social services? Kayleigh would never do that. Could she really get a council flat? It sounded highly unlikely. They would find her a hostel, or persuade her into an abortion.

My mind went back to the day I first knew I was pregnant. No off-the-shelf tests in those days. You had to go to the doctor to be sure, and when I had gone I was told that it was really too early to be certain. I should come back in a month. But I had known. Not just the missed periods, unlike Kayleigh, I kept careful records. It was a feeling of life bubbling about inside me, making all sensations sharper, showing the true colours of everyday objects: the yellowness of a field of buttercups rejected by the cows, the pink of a hayfield in June. I'd felt I was in the control of something greater than myself, my life taken over by a greater life. My whole being was engaged in a battle for this unseen embryo, with its tiny monster head, which was taking me over. I could feel it smiling, appreciating all I was doing for it. I went out into the night and told Gran above. I wished Gran could have been there. But I was sure that, wherever she was, Gran knew. I could feel her sharing the joy. It mattered less if Mother or Father knew. I hoped for a girl, to call Lily after Gran.

I had wanted to share this intense joy in the little pink tadpole, utterly dependent on me, put there by Husband, but mine now, only mine. When I told Husband, he had only said, 'Wait until the doctor says so.'

'I can feel it.'

'Nonsense. You can't feel it for weeks, Maude. Months.'

'Not its movement. Its existence. I feel I have life inside me. I feel more alive because it's there.'

I had felt like the Virgin Mary, and magnified the Lord I didn't believe in. I was blessed. The mighty would be put down from their seats, the humble and meek exalted. Life had seized me, as it had seized the Virgin Mary, and Kayleigh. I knew Kayleigh's pregnancy should be terminated, yet felt unreasonable joy, and groundless hope at this annunciation.

The girls were still fantasising about making the Shack into a home. I didn't want to interrupt them, but felt a growing sense of responsibility as an adult, which surprised me. I hadn't felt like an adult for years. It felt good. I almost saw the Shack as a possible home and had to tell myself it wasn't, could not be, realistic.

I realised it was up to me to find a sensible solution. How could I? I hadn't done anything sensible for years. I felt a huge weight of responsibility for the Krew, which I didn't want, couldn't cope with. I didn't want to get involved in their problems, but I was involved. What could I do?

Kayleigh was saying, 'I'm gonna leave home, right. Be by myself. Get well away from me mum. I'll go to the council, right, they'll give me a flat.'

'They'd want to know where you live first. They'd tell your mum,' said Suze.

'There's hostels and things, innit,' said Brenda.

'Nah. I'm not going near no social workers and all that fucking lot.'

'They'd take it into care,' said Sam. 'You can't have that. Know what I means?'

The discussion went on and on, round and round in circles. I was getting bored, thinking I should be going home; Pain was doing horrible things to my back again. Kayleigh would come to her senses in time. A fourteen year old couldn't have a baby, just like that. Adults would have to know. Her parents had a right to know, whatever Kayleigh thought about them. All this talk was fantasy. The girls lived on that borderland between fantasy and reality, as if they didn't quite know which was which. I started to get up off the milk crate, realising as I did that Kayleigh was crying bitterly. Weeping for a life. 'Me baby needs me to have it. There must be something I can do like. Somewhere I can go.'

No one said anything. Suze went and put her arms round her. Kayleigh cried louder.

'What am I to do? I wants this baby more than I've ever wanted anything in all me life, right. I can't get rid of it. I can't have them social workers, Mum, interfering. Know what I means? What the fuck can I do?'

Half of me thought that Kayleigh was behaving like a spoilt child, who needed a good smack; the other half felt she was right, the child had a right to life, Kayleigh should be allowed to bring it up as best she could. I was, nevertheless, appalled to hear myself saying, 'You could have it at my house.'

Kayleigh stopped crying, like the spoiled child when chocolate is offered.

'Does you really fucking mean that, Mau?'

Did I mean it? I'd no idea why I'd said it. I needed to say I hadn't meant it. Then why had I said it? They'd all heard me. What could I say now?

'I've got a house with two bedrooms, and only me to live in it. You can have the boys' room, and share the rest of the house.'

That was not what I meant to say.

'Really?' said Kayleigh.

'Really,' I heard myself say.

Kayleigh rushed over and put her arms round me, nearly knocking me over, and kissed me. When had I last been kissed? Kayleigh was the last of the girls I would have chosen to come and live with me. But I seemed to have invited her. I still couldn't understand why.

'I've been on my own for years,' I said. 'It's a bit of a mess. We'll have to clear it up, do a bit of cleaning. Clear Michael's things out of his room.'

What was I saying? What was I doing?

I was startled by a loud bang, an explosion somewhere on the other side of the rails. Gunfire? Surely not. Guns had not yet reached this city, although the girls talked sometimes of knifings. Probably just some old banger backfiring. Possibly a firework. I walked away slowly.

* * *

'It's only a firework. Soon be November the fifth. Try and go back to sleep ... No, dear, you need the drip, you were very dehydrated when they brought you in.'

Dehydrated. That's what I wanted to be. Dry. Dust to dust. But now I'm so, so thirsty.

'Don't worry, Maude.'

Why not? I've worried all my life.

* * *

I remember how worry was my constant companion throughout my years of motherhood. Michael's first day at school: would he wet himself? I remember the school gate mothers, with whom I spent many happy hours, sharing and avoiding the unvoiced fears of all mothers. Had I always known that motherhood was too good to last, must come to a bad end? As the boys grew older and walked to and from school on their own, I worried daily until they came home. Later still, as teenagers, I worried that they wouldn't return in the evenings, a worry which proved well-founded. Worry's sulphurous smell would invade my throat, his dry taste (raw sloes with vinegar) filled my mouth. He changed his shape to suit the occasion: sometimes he completely enveloped me, overcame me, sometimes he just stuck his sharp tentacles into me. He moved out when Grief arrived, with Michael's death.

When your worst fears, fears you have worked so hard to push to the back of your mind, become reality, look you in the face, jeer at your worry, worry becomes irrelevant. All that energy put into worry, all that effort, constantly checking and re-checking; in a single moment a life's work can come to nothing.

I'll never forget Michael's funeral, the worst day of my life. It was funeral cold, despite the mockingly bright sunshine. Travelling to the graceless crematorium with its smell of death, in the hearse, behind the coffin, I couldn't believe that this shiny box contained my lovely, lively son. We had expected to see very few at the crematorium. We hadn't informed his school friends; his boss knew he was dead, but hadn't asked about the funeral.

I was young, had not been to enough funerals to know the rules. I screamed the whole way to the crematorium. I can still taste those tears, like no tears I had shed before or since. Tart, acrid, grief-filled. When the hearse finally reached the crematorium, hidden away in a backstreet out of sight of as much of life as possible, the long car turning with difficulty into the narrow gate, I saw a huge congregation of parked motorbikes.

'Bikes!' I screamed. 'I never want to see another motorbike as long as I live. Do we have to go this way?'

'We're there now,' said Husband. I became hysterical. He tried to calm me. I didn't want to calm down.

'I can't bear it. I can't bear it.'

We followed the coffin slowly into the chapel, heard the chosen music sounding so inappropriate. I sank into the seat I was led to. Husband put his arm around me, and I shook it off. I shut my eyes, and concentrated on Grief. After a few moments I was aware that the little chapel was crowded. I turned round and saw the back seats were full of young men in leather jackets carrying crash helmets. It was the motor bikers, not a hallucination.

I jumped up and screamed, 'What are you doing here? Leave us in peace. Go away!'

'Hush, Ma,' said John, appearing from nowhere. 'They've come to the funeral.'

'It's our funeral? What right have they to be here?'

'They've come to say goodbye to Michael. They're his friends.'

'He'd be alive now if it weren't for them.'

There was some shuffling at the back.

'Do you know these people?' I asked John.

'Some of them. Slightly. They're good people, Ma. Michael's friends. He'd want them here.'

'He never told me.'

'You never listened.'

'I couldn't. I knew that bike would be the death of him. I was right.' The fresh tears were almost triumphant.

The taped music faded away, the parson stood up.

'We will sing hymn number ...' An organ started. Everyone except me got up. I heard lugubrious male singing from behind me, as I sat weeping.

When it was over at last, we shuffled slowly out into the cold sun, more inappropriate music following us. I wanted to get away, away from this place of death, where the mourners for the next funeral were greeting each other with those kisses kept for people we do not normally kiss. Few of them were dressed in black, chatting, laughing nervously, inappropriately. How could they laugh in such a place? A small child was crying; someone, who could have been an uncle, and who was obviously not in the habit of picking up small children, picked him up, and he screamed. Why bring a small child to such a place? What could his parents be thinking of?

A woman took the child and, while the uncle had been making soothing noises, she shouted, 'Will you be quiet. What will Granddad think?'

'Granddad's dead.' He stopped crying, just as everyone from both funerals was listening to him.

Granddad and Michael, both. But Granddad must have been old. Michael would never be old, never be a dad let alone a granddad. I began to list all the things he would never do, never be, as the noisy tears flowed.

Gran's funeral had been sad, but it had been a timely death. She was buried not burnt, that made it easier: earth to earth, Gran's had been an earthy life. There was a grave to visit, not just a plaque marking where ashes were. Gran's death removed a wellspring of strength that had been there for me since my childhood, but I had always known, though never considered, that Gran would not be there for ever. My tears for Gran flowed like rivers that cleansed and healed me, as my tears for Michael could not.

Father had organised Mother's funeral; her death had been generally accepted as a 'merciful release'. For Father any expression of emotion was weakness, shameful. So we all controlled ourselves at that funeral. When Father died, I arranged the funeral; once again the sadness was muted. He had had a 'good innings', been a good man, never been drunk, or stopped for speeding; he left little behind apart from his children. We cleared his flat: the canaries went to a pet shop, the clothes to Oxfam, the furniture, which had been Mother's choice, to a charity for the homeless. After a few weeks the world resettled around the space he had left, as if he had never been. But he had been. There was a space.

All funerals are the same, I thought, however different. Funeral friends and relatives, who knew the deceased in different roles come together. Some do not know each other, others, like Babs, wish they did not. Enforced politeness; not knowing where to look; nervous laughter restraining tears. Some emotions cannot be taken to a crematorium: sorrow is safe, tears are acceptable, sobs less so, open weeping is to be avoided, nothing showy, except the flowers. We must obey the crematorium rules: be seemly, look down, avoid the faces of others who don't know where to look, above all avoid seeing the tall chimneys, which will carry the loved one up into the ether, to mingle with all that is. Down here, wrapped in our private griefs, we fear the time when our smoke will mingle there.

The religious comfort themselves with certainties, which those who don't normally bother with religion borrow for the afternoon and then discard. A life has touched them, however slightly, touched the lives of all those present. All are changed by the life that is no more. We leave the crematorium once more smiling; laughter at the party can be louder. We eat greedily, reminding ourselves that we still can eat.

One of the motor bikers approached me, cutting short my silent monologue.

'I'm sorry if we upset you. We just wanted to say goodbye to Mickey. We were gutted at his death.'

'Gutted? Mickey? Who's Mickey?'

'Michael. He was a good mate.'

'He was my son, Michael. Not Mickey. But for you lot he'd be alive today.'

'You can't blame them, Ma,' John said, into the awkward silence.

'Bikes, bikers. If he'd only listened to me ...'

'He had to live his own life, Ma.'

'But he didn't. He's lost it.'

I broke out in renewed sobs. John put an arm around me, and supported me as I almost fell to the ground. 'You don't understand. You can't understand.'

'He was my brother, Ma.'

'I was his mother.'

'You're still my mother, Ma.'

I looked at him as if I didn't recognise him through the tears. He and Husband helped me to the waiting car. As it drove away the bikers relaxed, I thought I heard them laughing. How could they? First they killed my son, then they laughed.

I returned to the present on the Tip, realising that I'd been sitting too long and too still on the low milk crate. Pain made me cry out as I struggled up. The girls didn't hear my cry. They were giggling about some suggestive TV ad. I knew I was right in my determination never to get over Michael's death. Grief changes over time, grows rancid, distorted. Emotions harden. Everything doesn't pass. Time doesn't heal.

I had searched frantically through all the family albums finding photographs of Michael at every age, had them enlarged, expensively framed. Husband hated this, said he wanted to forget – how could one forget a child, pretend he never existed? I wanted to celebrate what he had been. Husband started going out more with men friends, work colleagues, drinking, so when he came home he was in no state to talk. One day he snatched up the photographs and hurled them into the waste-paper basket, saying something about drinking to forget, and coming home to be reminded. Now, so many years later, I could begin to understand. Having lived with Grief for so long, I began to realise he comes in varying guises.

When Husband left Grief was joined by Emptiness. Emptiness paralysed me: how could I fill the endless days when both sons and Husband had gone? At first I thought I should try to find some link with other people: evening classes, that sure route to human company. The first two I joined were cancelled for lack of support. 'The Twentieth Century Novel' was popular. Unfortunately, having once been a librarian, I knew more about the subject than the lecturer, who ignored the rudeness of the other students, when they made it clear they weren't interested in my views. I joined a rambling group, and then tried early morning swimming. I had brief conversations with other walkers, and listened in to the talk between friends in the swimming pool. Listening in, I shared a tiny portion of their lives, which was comforting in a lonely way. I participated surreptitiously, uninvited, in their lives, yet I knew I shared nothing. Nothing now made me feel alive.

I wondered about doing voluntary work.

'What do you have in mind?' asked the woman behind the desk.

'Helping people.'

She gave me a form to fill in and bring back. It asked all sorts of questions I couldn't begin to answer. Someone who knew me well had to give a reference. I didn't know anyone well, my friends had been Husband's friends, and disappeared with him. I was absolutely alone. I didn't want to help people, I wanted help. I was helpless. Had I filled in the form I would have been rejected as unsuitable: I was unsuitable.

Finally I surrendered to Grief as my only companion, and to permanent uselessness, living for my cats and my memories. I lost contact with people, stopped replying to neighbours' friendly 'good mornings', until they stopped saying it. I wept dry the empty space that became my life. I thought of ending it, but hadn't the courage. Grief approved: that would be too easy.

Would Husband have left me even if Michael hadn't been killed? Was there a girl, young enough to be his daughter, young enough to be excited about attracting him? I'd given up bothering about attraction even before the Tragedy: we were a married couple after all, taken each other for better or for worse, growing older and unattractive was all part of the worse. I accepted that he would no longer bring me flowers, remember my birthday or our anniversary, and assumed that he similarly accepted my ageing body. Yet once he stormed at me saying, 'I hate looking at you at the breakfast table. I see an ageing woman. I will not, I refuse to grow old.'

I almost laughed at his arrogance. How would he have faced old age and death without the Tragedy? Perhaps it brought back his first bereavement? His Children's Home didn't encourage their inmates to contact parents, and he'd never wanted to know who his parents had been. When I tried to encourage him, in the early days of our marriage, to ask about them, he had grown angry. The Home was his family, and soon we had our own family. He didn't need to know. Arrogantly, I thought my roots were strong enough for us both, but mine, too, were damaged when I went to live with Gran.

I remember once, in the Forest, seeing holes dug by badgers on a slope immediately beneath a mature beech tree. The roots were exposed, a shallow cave with a sandy floor was hollowed out where roots should be. How long could the tree stand, proud and straight as the others? It seemed to be desperately clinging on to its ancient life, as erosion washed more of its stony soil away. Where did Kayleigh's Krew have their roots? On the Tip? I had severed my root system, after the Tragedy. Could I find new roots here?

Why did I return to the Tip day after day?

Was I looking to find new roots? I had roots still in the Forest. Something of the Forest was part of me then, and still runs in my blood, like a river hiding in a deep ravine. Perhaps something of the miners' gritty determination helped to carry me through the long years of aloneness. Once long ago, Granddad had taken me back to visit the Forest, in that bumpy side-car, while Gran clung for her life on to his comforting back. Motorbikes had been fun then, but Gran insisted that they get the little bubble car, when my stay seemed likely to be indefinite.

In the war the Forest had become threatening, live ammunition was stored among the trees, surrounded by barbed wire, and fierce warnings: 'DANGER', or 'WAR DEPARTMENT. KEEP OUT.' A few children who couldn't read, or didn't care, were killed. We were no longer allowed to walk up the hill to the tree nurseries, with their long low thatched buildings, whose wire mesh walls guarded brown acorns and beech nuts, each bursting with the life of a great tree. A love of trees and their rootedness became part of me. I knew the pain of being uprooted … In all my days of aloneness I had never returned to the Forest, but held within me memories of its brooding, suspicious inhabitants, its picnic scented bracken and the ragged sheep roaming free, by ancient right. I remembered the summer silent stillnesses, when no birds sing, the impenetrable dense green of its canopy, brass bands, church fêtes, fancy dress parades and the Sunday evening charabanc loads of Welshmen, who came to drink and to sing in

English pubs when those in Wales were closed. 'Bread of Heaven' meant it was nearly time for them to get back into their coaches, crates of beer under the seats, and go down the steep twisting road back to Wales. Then I could go to sleep …

I remember how we eventually brought baby Mark home from hospital, in the taxi. Kayleigh was still shaky on her legs, having done none of the exercises prescribed by the physiotherapist, and thrown away the leaflet. 'I feels all lumpy,' she said. We travelled down in the lift.

'Lumpy?' said Suze. 'You've lost your lump.'

Kayleigh tried to laugh, it came out like half a laugh, half a cry. 'He's turned me into a fucking lump. I feels like jelly. I knows I looks a right mess.'

'So what's different?' said Suze.

'Give yourself time,' I said, trying to be the peacemaker.

The taxi finally drew up outside my house. Kayleigh got up with difficulty from the soft seat and eased herself out, like an old woman. Kayleigh looked at Mark, to make sure he was still there, then said, 'Home, Mark.' I breathed a sigh of relief. Home. We all moved indoors, then stood around awkwardly not knowing what to do next.

Kayleigh collapsed into the settee; I settled myself down next to her, saying, 'Put the kettle on, Suzie, there's a love, I'm desperate for a cup of tea.'

A loud banging on the front door brought Suze rushing out, 'Shush, you'll wake him.'

'Sorry,' whispered Kat. She and Sam were the first home visitors.

Mark didn't stir. I remembered being told to let them get used to sleeping in a noise. It makes life easier later on. I was getting quite good at not passing on good advice.

Kat hadn't visited the hospital. 'Can't stand hospitals, too much like jails. Take away your freedom.'

'But they make you better, not worse,' I said.

'Sometimes.'

Kat pushed past Suze and looked at Mark, now lying in his pink lined Moses basket.

'Can I hold her?'

'Yeah. But it's him not her.'

'I forgot. He do look like a girl. You wouldn't think a boy could be so tiny, innit.'

She picked up the child, so pale and soft, in her large black arms, and walked around making crooning noises, words which only Mark could hear. Kayleigh watched. I watched Kayleigh.

Mark, who had slept for some hours, now stirred and sensed something was different. The warm, claustrophobic, sterile atmosphere in which he had spent the first few days of his life, had changed to somewhere altogether more dangerous. He wriggled his mouth as he sought the comfort of Kayleigh's milk, but found only Kat's alien flesh. He stretched, filled his lungs with the unaccustomed air and began to wail, more loudly than ever before, louder even than that first cry of protest as he was separated from Kayleigh.

'Hush, hush, Baby,' said Kat, as she sat down next to Kayleigh, who took him and lifted up her jumper.

'He wants his fucking titty.'

Instantly Mark quietened as he sensed the milk. Kayleigh guided his tiny face to her breast; silence filled the room.

'Sorry I woke him,' whispered Kat.

'It's OK,' said Kayleigh. 'Me boobs is full o' milk.' Tiny milky noises filled the silence.

I watched Kayleigh's face: inscrutable. Was that love? Could all be well? She couldn't give up Mark now, could she? Worry laughed at me. Of course she could. Colic. Teething. Broken nights. Cracked nipples. How could a fifteen year old cope with all this? Toddler tantrums, the 'terrible twos', or was it 'terrible threes'. Both, as I remembered. Would she cope?

'Like hell,' said Worry.

Perhaps Kayleigh could go to that centre, get some GCSEs and A levels, go to college, find a nursery for Mark, and a well-paid job. I saw a bright future for them both, with my support. Kayleigh would blossom; I watched her feeding Mark now, surely love was gradually unfolding. With her intelligence and the good sense of one who has survived, the future was bright. Kayleigh would cope. She was a coper.

The vision was short lived, as Kayleigh transferred the child from one breast to the other, he vomited all over her.

'Ugh', Kat and Brenda recoiled.

'You ungrateful fucker.' I heard a frightening harshness

behind the words. 'If you keeps on doing that I'll take you back to the hospital.'

'He's had a big upset for one so small, coming here,' I said.

'Yeah, but look at me sweater.'

Mark, oblivious, was now sucking Kayleigh's other breast.

'You can't give him away,' said Sam.

'I can and all. He's mine, and there's plenty of people as wants babies and can't have 'em.'

My vision changed to foster homes, a troubled childhood, a problem child. Fighting. Worry. Guilt. I saw Kayleigh return to her mother, cursed, then forgiven, falling back into her old ways, failing at school, repeating all her mother's mistakes, and unsatisfactory relationships. Living her whole life on the margins of society.

I didn't see the third vision: adoption by loving, caring parents, with much to give. I was too busy thinking how I must do all in my power to support Kayleigh, help her to make a success of her life and Mark's. It was not in my power; Mark held the power. I tried to visualise Mark aged ten, and realised that I would probably not be there. Neither of my parents had reached their eighties. How would Kayleigh cope without me?

I owed so much to Kayleigh and her Krew. And to Gran. Without this house I would surely have died on the streets years ago, or on the Tip. Gran had left it to me, but I'd never made a will. Would they find John on my death, so that it could be his? Where was John? He must have a home: this house was not his. It was Kayleigh's and Mark's. Tomorrow I would see a solicitor.

Mark rejected the breast and began to cry.

'I think he may've poohed,' said Kayleigh, 'What'll I do?'

'You'll have to change his nappy; they showed you how,' I said. Could she really be so stupid?

'I've forgotten. You do it.'

I had watched the demonstration, remembered that the pretty bit had to be at the front, but had not taken in the details of changing disposable nappies. Michael's and John's terry nappies blew daily in the breeze in the garden. I remembered smelling their freshness, and the smell of the steam that filled the house on wet days, when they were dried on the fire-guard. These efficient, sterile pieces of plastic and Velcro frightened me.

'I'll help,' said Suze. Kayleigh struggled with the stiff poppers on the sleep suit. Mark's head fell off her knee, and hung down, his cries grew louder.

'You need to put him on his changing mat,' said Suze, laying out the plastic object, unknown to me; I had always changed my babies on my knee. Kayleigh picked up the now screaming Mark and plonked him on the cold plastic, where he cried louder still. How could one so small make so much noise? I watched. The tiny tummy button, where the placenta had only recently fallen off, was the permanent sign that he had once been part of Kayleigh, and always would be. I remembered Michael's and John's little indentations with their unique whorls and folds of skin, like the irregular rings in the trunk of a tree. I was now too stiff to see my own, but knew I had once been a part of Mother, as father had of Gran. Nothing can take that belonging away.

'You'll need a wipe, innit.' Brenda opened the plastic box and drew out a string of damp pieces of material, with difficulty separating one off and holding it out to Kayleigh.

'Hang on, hang on. I can't do it all at once. And you,' she said to Mark, 'you shut your fucking mouth. Can't you see I'm doing me best?'

I remembered cotton wool, moistened in a saucer of warm water then flushed down the loo with the contents of the nappy, which went into an enamel bucket of disinfected water, to be washed next day. It had all been so much simpler in my day, even if there was more to be done. Sam took the dirty nappy outside, the lid of the wheelie bin slammed shut, it would have to wait a week now to join all the other debris of life on the rubbish tip. The room was quiet, as we all took in just how much this baby would change our lives; the muffled barking of a dog came through the closed window.

* * *

Do I hear hysterical barking? Is it a dog putting an end to my peace? No dogs here, they keep reassuring me. No dogs here. No peace either. I would like to sleep.

'Try and get some sleep, Maude.'

How can I sleep in all this noise?

I try to say, 'Could you please turn that alarm thing off? And the light.'

She's gone again.

That's what I'm trying to do: get some sleep. Sleep doesn't come with trying. Somehow, a dog has taken away my chance of that most peaceful of sleeps.

Sleep that knits up the ravelled sleeve of care. What does that mean? Did I care for Kayleigh? Is its sleeve ravelled? Unravelled?

In that sleep of death what dreams may come. I think I was quite close to death, but there were no dreams.

I can't sleep here.

All I want is peace: the grand peace of the Moor, ancient, splendid, in the early morning light.

I must have slept. Not a peaceful sleep. Barks invade my dreams. Dreams of struggling with dogs. Of wild barking. When I open my eyes it's to another voice urging me to eat. A smell of gravy fills the air. I shake my head, and try to go back to sleep. But there's no peace in sleep here, only in death. My problems return to me slowly, then faster. I curse that dog.

Sleep. I lie waiting for that unreal half waking sleep, which was all I had until Kayleigh arrived.

* * *

I remember how in those far off days of grief, when I woke I never seemed fully awake: in sleep part of me was still awake, keeping watch over my dangerous unconscious. I never dreamed. Years ago I had willed myself not to dream, for fear I might dream that Michael was alive. I couldn't bear the thought of the waking realisation that it had been a dream, that he was dead. It would be like losing him all over again. That would be unbearable, once was more than enough. Now, dreams were beginning to hover at the edge of my sleep, flying as I woke. Sometimes I managed to hold on to them long enough for a fleeting impression. That recurring childhood dream returned, of being chased by a herd of cows down a steep hill at the bottom of which was a railway line with a train approaching. I remembered it from seventy years ago: the realisation that there was no escape. Sleep is treacherous. What secrets might it reveal? What dire messages? Safer not to let go completely.

Dreams, I thought, are night-time wakefulness, out of place, out of time. No time or place for thoughts, and the fears that thought brings: the fear of fears. Dreams are so quick to fade, perhaps we should not know our dreams, they are rightly hidden from us. In the dark of the night, we can confront our ultimate fear without recognising it. Only fragments pursue us into wakefulness: do we exist at all? Are we no more than a dream? A nightmare? Sleep does not come …

I remember the night, long ago, when Michael returned to me. Woken by a draught, I got up, closed the window and got back into bed. Husband made a complaining noise; I tried to go back to sleep, but then I smelled him. Michael had always smelt, strongly or faintly depending on how recently he had bathed or changed his clothes, of motorbike oil. The room was filled with that scent now, with an undertow of his aftershave: I sat up and drank it in. In the past I'd hated it, was always asking, telling, him to wash. Now it was the best perfume I'd ever smelled. I took in deep breaths of it, then woke Husband.

'Can you smell him?'

'Smell what?'

'Michael.'

'Don't be so stupid. Go back to sleep, you silly woman.' As he turned over and over, getting comfortable, the smell slowly faded, and I wished I'd not woken him. Michael would have lingered longer for me alone; he had surely come for me alone. I realised then that there would never be any comfort from Husband.

Sometimes people who had also lost children said to me, in the days when people still spoke to me, 'Part of me died the day he died.' Not for me. Michael still lives in me. I am changed for ever, but nothing of me died. That would have been too easy. Grief, tinged mysteriously with a morbid satisfaction, changed with the passing years but would never go away. Grief folded his cold arms around me, protecting my pain ...

I remember how exasperation, mixed with tenderness, drove me to the hospital the day after Mark was born. They said any time after ten. I waited until ten past for the twenty minute walk, putting on the new coat I had bought at the 'Mind' shop for the pre-birth meeting. It wasn't really cold enough for a thick coat, but it was respectable. As I walked I remembered dressing carefully for that meeting with midwife, social worker, health visitor, doctor and Kayleigh. All had Kayleigh's best interests at heart, and, after initial uneasiness, I believed that they really did. Kayleigh had been on her best behaviour. Perhaps it would have been better had they not taken me at my word when I said I was 'in loco parentis'. My BBC English, and a certain authority I used to use with those who returned their library books late, made my story convincing. No one doubted that Kayleigh wanted to keep her baby, and they all did their best to make it possible. Even Kayleigh, who had been terrified of this meeting with the massed ranks of 'Them', was persuaded that they cared about her baby. And about her. Only the suggestion that she should attend a centre for teenage girls with babies and continue her education, had threatened consensus. They finally agreed to leave this until after baby was born. What were they all going to say now?

I walked briskly, hardly feeling the pain in my knee, wondering if Kayleigh's maternal instincts had surfaced during the night. I half wanted to take Kayleigh by the shoulders and shake her saying, 'You said you'd love him!' Of course she hadn't; she'd expected 'her'. The other half wanted to fold her in my arms and wash her in tears.

I stopped at the traffic lights. The red man changed to green, but I didn't notice, was deaf to the insistent bleeping, urging me to cross. I realised I loved Kayleigh: why had I only just seen this? I loved her fiercely, not as the daughter I never had, but for who she was. The lights changed again, and I felt the exasperation, tenderness and gratitude of my love; love that was the product of Kayleigh's need, and Baby's helplessness. A different love from mine for the boys, not founded on the fickle, instinctive maternal love that Kayleigh seemed to lack. Of course I would happily go to prison for her. The sun shone on the traffic lights, so that both green and red seemed on together.

'Watch out, lady,' said a loud male voice, dragging me back as the cars flowed in front of me. I looked up at the bored face, mumbling thanks. The young man ignored me: he could be Baby's father.

I crossed carefully when the green man urged me on, but had to wait again at the level crossing. I peered down the line: there was the Tip, the Shack was out of sight. A train rumbled slowly past, gently shaking the cold air. The gates didn't open. Another long wait. I could see the grey height of the hospital as an unbelievably long freight train crossed. My impatience grew: how many trucks? What was in them all? Where were they going? Why? Some bore the mysterious words, 'not to be loose shunted'. What was loose shunting? The sun shone on the lines, but still the gates remained closed. Was something wrong with them? The traffic built up behind, the air filled with fumes and another train, a short rail car, covered in garish advertisements, pulled slowly out of the station making its leisurely way over the crossing. Why had we waited so long for so unimportant a train? Hardly had it gone when a long distance train slowed and passed. So many empty first class coaches, then the refreshment car, adding a faint whiff of coffee to the diesel fumes. When it had gone the crossing raised its arm reluctantly, and the impatient pedestrians and cyclists moved, followed by the long line of cars and lorries, which went on to cause a blockage at the next roundabout.

I hurried with fear and joy to the hospital, followed the signs to maternity. 'I've come to see Kayleigh,' I told the disembodied voice from the buzzer, 'I'm her aunty.' I was so much more than an aunty. Why ever hadn't I said I was Kayleigh's mother? It was not much more untrue. The door clicked and I was again enveloped in that chemical, unemotional concern. I hurried straight to Kayleigh's room. Suze was there; both girls were sitting on the bed, eating chocolate. Baby lay peacefully in his cot. I realised I'd brought no present for him, no flowers for Kayleigh. But if I went to the hospital shop now I would have to pass those official inquisitive eyes again. Flowers could wait.

Kayleigh and Suze turned as I opened the door. Resisting the urge to smother Kayleigh with kisses, I put my arm gently round her shoulder, 'How are you?'

'I'm well fucked.'

I resisted asking, 'How's Baby?'

There was a long pause. Baby, professionally wrapped in his spotless cot, whimpered and went back to sleep. Neither girl took any notice. I looked at Kayleigh, her unhappy face showed no sign of maternal love, her eyes dark ringed, her hair a mess.

'How did you sleep?'

After a long pause, 'They took the baby away. But there was all that noise all night. Banging and shouting. Babies crying all over. How are you expected to sleep in all that?'

She fell back exhausted, Suze moved protectively closer. Slightly muffled hospital noises filled the air.

'I wants to go home,' said Kayleigh, almost too quietly for me to hear.

My heart lifted up to join the seagulls high over the hospital, then sank, torpedoed by the possibility that she meant her mum's home. No one noticed Baby's whimpering, which now became a cry. After a few minutes I picked him up. Baby recognised my long unused experience and fell silent again. Suze watched as I rocked the child gently.

'How d'you do that?' she asked.

'I've no idea,' I said. 'I think he's hungry.' Baby was trying to find something to suck.

'The nurses'll feed him,' said Kayleigh.

He'd rather you did, hung unsaid between Kayleigh and me. Baby's hand found its way to his mouth, and for a while that contented him. I watched his eyes screwing themselves up for a cry. He desperately needed to feel that the world was a caring, loving place: he needed a mother. Suze got up and gazed at the bundle, 'Aah,' she said: that 'Aah' that is only said to babies.

Kayleigh ignored all three of us, put another chocolate in her mouth and lay down, turning her back on us, crying out loud in pain as she did so.

'A fucking boy. All that for a boy. If I'd known he were a boy I'd have had him got rid of.'

'He'll be glad you didn't one day,' I said.

'You can't know that.'

Kayleigh and Suze snuggled down in the bed. Kayleigh wept. I worked hard at not interfering. Kayleigh fell asleep at last, and Suze finally went home. I accepted the offer of a cup of tea, but not the suggestion that I should go home and get some rest. 'All will be well.' The words swam into my mind, from somewhere in the past. Could all be well? I was too exhausted to think. I fell deeply asleep in the tall, hard chair, and dreamed of other births, other deaths. Husband and John came to me, unsure if they were dead or alive. Michael came briefly, to say, 'I'm sorry, Mum.' John, with his wife, (or was it his widow?) came with three small daughters, who grew up before my eyes, and roared away on motorbikes. Husband begged to come back.

'You'll need someone to care for you now you're growing old.'

'Speak for yourself.'

A fit of cramp woke me, I cried out, as the dreams scattered. A nurse came running, rubbed my leg and offered me another cup of tea.

'Bit of a character, your niece.'

'She's not really ...' I began, then, woken by the shock of what I had almost said, continued 'ready for motherhood. A child herself. I despair of her mother. She's had a hard life ...' Not quite sure who I meant.

'Who hasn't? She's lucky to have you.'

'Her mother all but threw her out.'

'Why was she so sure it would be a girl?'

'She just assumed. No one told her.'

'Did they tell her at the scan that it was a girl?'

I tried to remember. Kayleigh had said something like, 'Look at her.'

'Her?'

'Yeah, got no willy,' Kayleigh had said.

'I can't see anything very much.' I remembered peering at the screen, screwing up my eyes as we watched the tiny wriggling creature in amazement.

Kayleigh had squirmed and giggled at the cold jelly, then marvelled at the blurred flickering picture of a strange bean like creature that seemed to be alive.

'Look at her, Mau.'

'I don't think it's a her,' I think the sonographer said, I still don't know what that means, but that's what the letter said.

'I knows it is,' said Kayleigh.

'When I had babies we had to wait until they were born to know if it was a boy or a girl. Knowing so long ahead must spoil some of the magic,' I said.

'Yeah, yeah, but I know this is a girl. I'm her mother, see. I'll love her. I thinks I'll call her Mary.'

'Bit old fashioned,' said Suze, when she heard. 'What if it's a boy?'

'It's not. It's Mary.'

Mary would have no father, like Mary in the Bible. If I'd believed in God I'd have said that God was the father. This would be a Child of the Holy Ghost. But I'd banished that white bearded man in the sky, who looked after sparrows, but never answered prayers, as I'd banished Father Christmas. Two lies told to children to prepare them for an unjust world.

Had the white coated woman with the magic wand been about to say something, then changed her mind? I remembered that she had been called away to the phone. When she returned she'd been full of indignation with a doctor who accused her of losing some files. He'd discovered them, and rang to tell her there was no need to go on looking.

'He didn't bother to apologise,' she said. 'Doctors!' She seemed to have almost forgotten us.

'Men,' I said …

But I couldn't really remember much. 'Do you think she'll come round?'

'I've seen it happen,' said the nurse.

My disappointment that my nursery would be occupied by yet another boy had vanished. I forgave the child its sex as quickly as I had forgiven Michael for not being a girl. But it might not be occupied at all if Kayleigh meant what she said. We all say things we don't mean, when we're in an emotional situation, I told myself.

'You need some proper sleep. Why don't you go home? We'll take care of Madam,' said the nurse.

'I want to be here when she wakes, in case I could help.'

Kayleigh had been so quiet for so long, lying lifeless, that I'd almost forgotten her, now I was aware of her stirring, sitting up, groaning, glancing at the cot.

'Still a fucking boy, then? It weren't a nightmare?'

'He's your baby. He's beautiful.'

I was overcome by feelings of great-aunthood; Baby's sex was irrelevant. Kayleigh was still Kayleigh. She turned her back on both me and Baby and wept. I went round the bed, and tried to put my arms round her.

'Fuck off!' I didn't move. 'And take that fucking baby with you.'

When I still didn't move, 'Git out of me room, can't you. I needs some peace and all.'

How could Kayleigh not want to scoop her child up into her love? A picture of myself fifty years ago sprang into my mind. I'd not wanted to be parted from Michael for one second. I felt further from Kayleigh then than at any time since she moved into my home. How could she not want to look at Baby? After all she had said about love.

'Git out!'

I went out and wandered down the corridor. Perhaps adoption would be best? Kayleigh could go home to her mum, I could … I thought of my clean house, of the nursery, so lovingly prepared, those dreadful Pooh curtains …

The Krew had transformed the boys' room into a garish nursery, with Walt Disney animals on the walls, a Pooh bear mobile hanging from the ceiling, looking so out of place against the tender pink walls, so 'sweet' to Kayleigh. I winced at this new Winnie the Pooh. Gran had taught me to love Pooh Bear, a love I'd tried unsuccessfully to pass on to my boys. He seemed to have become a tawdry cartoon character. His essential Poohishness sacrificed to popular appeal: less 'a bear with very little brain', more one of utter brainlessness. Could this empty creature, who was far too fat, a fat that obviously came from junk food not honey, have the agility to play Pooh-Sticks? Did children still play Pooh-Sticks?

What should I do for the best? Did it matter what I did? Was it all my fault, all done for my own selfish reasons? Questions I had refused to answer.

I sat by Kayleigh's bedside, when I realised she was asleep again. I watched, from the high hospital window, the silent city laid out below. Where once dock workers scurried with vital cargoes there was now a car park. I could see, but not hear, the gulls' cries unifying the city. These cries were heard by those in the prison round the corner, probably not by those who sleep their lives away between the night shelter and the day centre, around another corner, nor by those in the exclusive flats, which once were warehouses.

Changelessness underpinned the fast changing city: the river, the four main streets kept their ancient names of North, South, West and East, meeting at a cross, and the remains of one of the many ancient churches whose bells once rang across the city sky.

The streets were crossed by overhead roadways linking the ubiquitous car parks, like a rain forest canopy. The Cathedral tower proclaimed a certainty, a permanence, ignored by today's vain search for meaning. I hadn't been in the cathedral, or given it any thought, for years. Once, soon after the Tragedy, I had wandered in seeking an answer to my misery. I had found it cool; the hot sun, filtered through stained glass, cast rich colours indiscriminately on to floor, walls, pews and tourists. Its smells rose to the arched ceiling: fading lilies, candle wax and old, old, stone; the cold damp rising from the medieval floor. I had found no comfort there.

I could just see the river, which bounded the city to the West, as it had always done; today, after days of rain, it was swollen and brown, overflowing its banks, several fields were dressed up as lakes. It was flowing fast, dark with menace, bringing the rich Welsh soil down from the rainy hills, making its perilous way to the sea. It whirled and danced its dance of death, almost making the city an island.

The railway crossed the river on a long low bridge, taking it above the flooded fields and into the city, to the station, and on past the Tip, which I could see from my vantage point. The yellow ragwort was not yet out. Between the shiny lines hurrying away, I could see the tangles of rusty, long disused, tracks going nowhere, criss-crossing the Tip, invisible from the ground.

My eyes moved to the Shack. The Krew still met there occasionally, but this, too, would soon be left to decay unnoticed, like those redundant buffers. Steam, coal, furnace, had no place in today's world. This is not my century, I thought. Mine is part of the history I see below.

I paced the corridors for a while, peeping into other wards, watching mothers getting to know their babies. I went back; Suze was in bed with Kayleigh.

Suze, like me, had forgiven Baby his sex. 'He's beautiful.'

'He's a boy. How could I have done it?'

'He's perfect, Kayles. Look at his tiny fingers.'

'Boys' fingers.'

'Can I hold him?'

'You can have him for all I cares. Take him. Bring him up.'

'I'll help you to bring him up. He'll be different.'

Kayleigh looked at Baby for a brief second, doubtfully. The idea of bringing him up seemed just too much for her and she burst into tears again. Suze flung her arms around her, and cried too. Baby stirred in his sleep, and then joined Kayleigh, crying remarkably noisily for his size. Kayleigh was unmoved.

I watched them. What had I done? My deeply buried maternal instincts stirred, then took possession of me. I picked up the tiny bundle, cradling the flopping head, crooning.

'There, there, come to your Aunty Maude.' Long forgotten expertise returned. For a moment the child was quiet, as I put his head against my shoulder and started to pace the room rocking him.

Kayleigh noticed the crying had stopped and looked up. She and Suze stared. No one said anything for a long time, apart from my comforting noises, as the child whimpered faintly, unenthusiastically. I tried to put him back in his cot, but then the whimpering gave way to angry cries. I looked at the two girls on the bed.

'It's you he wants, not me,' I said gently, almost inaudibly. 'I think he's hungry.'

Kayleigh didn't move. To my surprise Suze held out her arms to the child and I carefully transferred him to her, showing her how to protect his head. Suze gazed down at Baby with a tenderness I was sure she had never felt before; this was the first time she'd held a baby. Kayleigh moved away from her, looked away.

'Kayles,' whispered Suze,' he's lovely.'

'He's a fucking boy,' said Kayleigh. She allowed herself another brief glance at her son, then looked away again.

Baby stopped crying temporarily, as Suze imitated my rocking.

'What's his name?'

'He ain't got one.'

'Give him one.'

'I don't want him.'

I sighed. 'You could still give him a name.'

'What for?'

I said, very quietly, 'You conceived him, you carried him for nine months, you gave him birth. Now you can give him a name.'

'I thought he were a girl. Mary. I'd never of carried him if I thought he were a boy.'

'You decided to keep him when you didn't know whether he was a boy or a girl.'

'I did know. I just knowed he were a girl. I'm not into boys. It were a fucking boy as landed me in this here mess.'

'He's only a baby,' said Suze. 'It's not his fault he's a boy.'

'It's not my fault neither. I can't be doing with boys.' Kayleigh was crying again with exasperation.

I looked from Kayleigh to Suze to the unwanted Baby. Kayleigh's eye moved to Baby, now crying loudly. She looked away, unconcerned. Another nurse came in.

'He wants his mum,' she said, taking Baby firmly from Suze.

'I'm not sure his mum wants him just yet,' I said.

The nurse tried to put Baby in Kayleigh's arms. 'Can you just sit up a bit more?'

'Nah.'

'Make a lap for him. Let's see if he'll feed. He sounds hungry.'

Kayleigh slithered under the bedclothes, 'Nah.'

'Come on,' coaxed the nurse, as if she were talking to a small child, which she was. 'He's a beautiful baby.'

'I don't want him.' Kayleigh's voice was muffled. Suze, the nurse and I stood looking at the quivering form in the bed. Baby screamed louder. No one said anything. Then Suze said quietly, 'She thought it was a girl.'

The nurse glanced at the notice above the bed. 'Kayleigh,' she coaxed again.

'Take him away.'

'He wants feeding.'

'You fucking feed him then.'

'He wants you.'

'Tough.' The bedclothes heaved, the sobs started again. Suze tried to hold Kayleigh's miserable, hidden body. The nurse looked at me questioningly. I shrugged, then she carried Baby away. His cries became fainter, then disappeared. I sat down to wait. After a while Kayleigh emerged from her crumpled bedding. Suze stroked her head.

'Has he gone?'

'Yes,' said Suze. 'You asked them to take him away.'

Kayleigh fell back on the pillows, her eyes wet, staring at the ceiling while we waited.

No one spoke for some time, then Kayleigh said, 'I could murder a coke.'

Suze stood up purposefully. 'I'll get you some,' she said, and disappeared. I moved my chair nearer to the bed before sitting down; Kayleigh continued to stare at the ceiling. I sat by her in silence.

At first it seemed an awkward silence, then Kayleigh began to relax into the quiet, accepting it, perhaps finding some comfort in it. I relaxed too, leaning closer to the bed, sharing the silence. Beyond the door we could hear the usual noisy hospital sounds: crying babies, hurrying purposeful feet, urgent voices, banging. Important, vital work was going on. I strained my ears and felt the pattern underlying all the clatter: a celebration of new life. I let it come slowly from the background into the quiet space, which was mine and Kayleigh's.

We were drawn together, with no part in the business beyond the door. Each could feel the sound of silent, sleeping babies, each drew it very differently into our shared silence. The quiet seemed to ease Kayleigh's pain. I felt, somehow, I had no idea how, all could eventually be well. Baby, away in the nursery, unaware of the dramas around his birth, chose life, greedily sucking from the tiny bottle.

Suze was gone a long time. The silence held us until she hurried in.

'Hospital shop's crap. Only had Pepsi. Had to run round to the corner shop, and they weren't much better. Smelly place. But they had coke.'

'Cheers,' said Kayleigh. A nurse came in and looked at us:

Suze gently stroking Kayleigh's forehead, me pausing for breath in the midst of a long battle, Kayleigh drinking coke, looking more belligerent than ever. The nurse thought better of whatever she had come in for, turned to Kayleigh, mumbling almost inaudibly, 'You all right?' and quietly left without waiting for a reply. Some time later she returned to say that it was rest time, the visitors must go, but could return later.

Kayleigh looked as if she were about to protest she didn't want a rest, but instead she flopped back heavily. 'See ya,' she said, adding, 'Ta for the coke.'

We left the ward. 'He's all right, isn't he, Maude?' said Suze.

'Lovely.' I was glad to be getting out of the hothouse atmosphere of the maternity ward, with its urgent purposefulness. All I wanted was to go home and sleep.

* * *

'Can I take your blood pressure, dear?' I nod. Be my guest. She wraps something round my arm, puts something on my finger, and in my ear. Reads dials and writes it all down.

'What's your name? Address? You're a long way from home. Does anyone know where you are?' I shake my head sadly. Tears decide to wash my eyes.

'Date of birth?'

I'm seventy five. Three quarters of a century. Not old by today's standards. Neither of my parents reached their three score years and ten. I've had a five year bonus. Who knows, had I learned to live in all those years I mourned, had I taken exercise, eaten healthily, made new friends after Husband left, I might now be fit and healthy. It was so long before I realised that my suffering was self-inflicted, and in vain.

'Does anyone live with you?'

I keep silent, then very quietly, 'Mark. Kay. Sometimes Sue.' She seems to have heard me.

'Your husband, daughters?'

I don't have the strength to laugh. Husband gone, these many years ago. No daughter. Sons gone too. Michael dead.

More questions, telephone number … I turn my back, and shut my eyes. But the peace has gone. For ever. I feel as helpless as poor Shellie.

* * *

I remember how on the Tip the girls used to discuss their parents' shortcomings. I found it hard to believe some of their stories: Kat's visits to her father in prison; Shellie's mother in and out of the psychiatric ward, Shellie was her carer; Tiger's altercations with her probation officer; brothers' delinquencies, drugs; parents' changing partners; Brenda's arson attempts. Such stories embellished, re-heated, were shared among us on the Tip, to accompanying murmurs of support, condolence, giggles or whatever seemed appropriate, as the irrelevant trains went by. I listened; unwilling to believe in mothers who cared so little for their children. You couldn't make it up, I thought.

I found I had some sympathy with Brenda, when she described the satisfaction of seeing living flames. I almost felt I understood. I remembered Gran's open fire, before the coming of the gas.

The girls seemed as comfortable with quiet as with giggling on the Tip. I found both embarrassing. Had John and Michael talked about Husband and me like these girls did of their parents? Had they been as scornful? Had there been the same ravine of misunderstanding between me and my boys? Had my family life before the Tragedy been lit by rose tinted spectacles, scented with quiet joy? Now all memories were overlaid by the grey cloud of the Tragedy, smelling sourly of decay and defeat. A gulf, like a mocking grin, opened up between me and Husband. Had that really not been there before? Surely he had not always contradicted everything I said, and I hadn't always found everything he said irritating?

The girls were no less dismissive of their teachers. I wouldn't like to have to teach them. I remembered my long forgotten ambition. Husband and I had both wanted to teach; neither my father nor Husband's Home encouraged education beyond sixteen. I had good exam results, better than Husband, but it was Husband who hated his work in the post office. So I supported us both for two years while he did a diploma in education at the local Teacher Training College. I loved my job at the library, loved Husband, and assumed that once he qualified it would be my turn. But we both wanted children, so my teaching was put off until they grew up, and then put off. The idea lost some of its appeal when Husband found there was more to teaching than Training College had suggested. Teaching practice, as a student under the supervision of the class teacher, was very different from being totally responsible for forty five nine year olds. Once in the classroom, he found he lacked an indefinable something, which the likes of Kayleigh and her Krew would instantly have recognised.

He went back to the post office when Michael arrived; he said he got more respect from the customers. Peace returned to our evenings. I put my energies into my own boys. Was it really not until Michael's death that it had all started to go wrong?

Kayleigh told me how she and Suze had each ended up at the same school: a sink school, the last choice of all parents who cared which school their children attended. Kayleigh had come to Suze's rescue in her first miserable days. She and Kayleigh were the only girls who knew no one else in the class. A silent chemistry, perhaps the attraction of opposites, drew them together. Kayleigh was flattered at Suze's attention, Suze was both terrified of, and filled with admiration for, Kayleigh. The Krew gradually formed itself around them. Staying in the Krew had become the most important thing for Suze. She at first resented no longer being Kayleigh's special friend, but if anyone suggested that Suze was too posh for the Krew,

Kayleigh would veto it. She became the leader, and it became 'Kayleigh's Krew', and they all seemed to accept it as natural. Other girls came and went; in year nine, numbers were dwindling as attracting boys was becoming all important. The Krew was for girls: girls who continued to see boys as a threat, they drew closer together.

Suze's Mother had chosen only grammar schools, when she filled in the secondary school choice form. When none of them selected her, Suze ended up, like Kayleigh, at the sink school. Mummy had gone down to the education department and argued. Daddy had gone down and shouted. They both encouraged Suze not to think of it as her school, pending their useless appeal.

Then Mummy went to see the head, worried about Susie's friendship with Kayleigh; she was cross at being fobbed off with the form teacher. 'Ms. Tucker knows her much better than me,' said the head. Kayleigh's reputation had preceded her from junior school, and Ms. Tucker had been alarmed when she found her in her class. She thought Suze was a good influence on Kayleigh.

'I don't send my daughter to school to help you with your problem children.' Mummy disapproved of Ms Tucker's make up, wondering why the Ms: neither one thing nor the other.

Ms. Tucker promised to keep an eye on them, and told the head when she realised that they were bunking off after registration.

Kayleigh told me how a social worker had turned up at her mother's door, asking why Kayleigh was not at school much of the time. A blazing row had followed, when Kayleigh said how much she hated the school and, rightly, accused her mother of not filling in the form for choice of secondary school. Her mother said she thought that if she did not bother Kayleigh would go to the nearest school. Unfortunately she also said that she knew Kayleigh would not want to go to the grammar school. This was the last straw for Kayleigh, she told her mother she didn't fill in the form because she didn't care. Swear words flew angrily through the air between them.

Finally Kayleigh banged out to the house and went back to the Tip, before Mum got violent. She didn't often get violent, but you couldn't be too careful. She'd been violent with Dad. That's one reason he'd fucked off. Kayleigh didn't blame him. Now that he was gone, and Mum had chucked Jason out, there was only her left to go on to. She said she told her mum that she was untidy, greedy, never told her where she was going, stayed out late, got up late. She didn't care what had happened to Jason. Kayleigh knew he'd been sofa hopping for a while; that meant he must spend nights between sofas in shop doorways. Serve Mum right if she went to jail because she didn't manage to get Kayleigh to school. Mum was for ever going on about how she'd carried her for nine months: that didn't mean she owned her. She hadn't asked her to. In fact, she could think of quite a few people she might have preferred to be carried by. What choice did she have? She was old enough to choose now: school was a waste of time. We listened to this and much more.

Another train rushed past, with its message of another world on the mainline. But on the sidelines where we lived, life could still bubble up like weeds that insinuate themselves between paving stones, defiantly flowering in impossible conditions. The girls were giggling again, evading the seagulls, questioning the certainties of the through trains. Trains played little part in their lives: they didn't have recurring nightmares of missing trains, running along platforms just in time to see the train disappear into the distance. Only Suze had regular holidays, and these involved cars and aeroplanes, not trains. She did not dare to admit to enjoying going abroad. There was much she couldn't admit to and be sure of keeping her place in the Krew.

The last time I had been on a train had been years and years ago, just after Husband left. I went to stay with my brother and Babs, in that dark town near Manchester, hoping vaguely to resume contact with my childhood family. My brother was still bitter.

'Why should you have that house, Maude? It was a family home, not Gran's to bequeath.'

'It was Gran's. And it was over twenty years ago.'

Everyone had assumed the house was rented. Granddad was fond of saying, 'This isn't going to pay the rent.' No one had realised that he'd bought it in the 1930s for a few pounds. Gran probably thought you paid rent on a house that belonged to you;

probably neither of them had heard the word mortgage. Granddad left it to Gran, who left it to me.

'Why Maude, for goodness sake?' Mother asked. I knew why, although I couldn't say. I remembered my anger and despair coming to live with Gran and Granddad in the city when Mother went into the sanatorium, jealous that my brother went to a near-by aunty, and did not have to leave my beloved Forest. That was where my roots were. Was that what the Krew lacked? Roots, that could bind them to society?

* * *

Roots dry up, wither away. I learnt that in the Forest. Can new roots form? How? They need watering. I need water. I've never been so thirsty. I wish I could reach my water.

'Can I have a drink?'

No one hears.

I can't reach my water jug.

* * *

I remember coming to the maternity ward that day. I was met by Sam coming out. Sam wanted me to 'talk some sense into her'.

She said, 'She's going to give that baby away. She can't. She can't.'

I tried to calm her. 'We don't know what she'll decide to do.'

'Well we've fucking gotta make sure she don't give him away. Can't you help? You understand me?'

'I don't want that either. But what can we do? We must wait. Kayleigh may come round and love him.'

'Maybe they won't give her time. He's a fucking baby, Mau, innit.'

She ran away crying. I found Kayleigh in tears also, leaning out of bed, staring at the tiny being in the cot. I sat down on the bed beside her, and put my arm round her. Kayleigh half sat up, snuggling against me, blowing her nose on the sheet. I passed her a tissue. She sniffed like a small child, moving further from Baby.

'Sam were here,' she said, after a long pause.

'Yes, I met her.'

Kayleigh's sobs died away, soon echoed by the pathetic cry of Baby. Kayleigh jumped; started crying again.

I picked up the child. 'There, there,' I said in my most soothing tones. 'There, there. Don't cry.' Unsure who the last was addressed to; Baby nestled comfortably in my arms. He was minute, yesterday's wrinkles seemed to have been washed away, his face now was pink. He yawned in a surprisingly adult way, stretched his limbs amazingly wide, relaxed as only babies and cats can, closed his eyes, and lay peeping out from time to time, viewing the world cautiously, not sure what to make of it. Kayleigh's sobs grew louder; she flung herself back on the pillows.

I spoke quietly to Baby, words of a love Kayleigh could not feel.

'What am I to do, Mau?'

I sat beside her, Baby up against my shoulder, and put my free arm round Kayleigh.

'Give yourself time, Kayleigh. You don't have to do anything until you feel stronger.' After a while, as Kayleigh's sobs slowed and became quieter, I cautiously took my arm away, moved Baby so that Kayleigh could see him. I felt, as Sam had, how could anyone not want to cuddle this tiny creature? Kayleigh did not. After a while she turned her head and allowed herself to look at her son. She stared in silence, her muscles tense, forbidding her to be moved by the child.

I managed to resist the temptation to say, 'Hold him.' I could feel the drumbeat of his heart sending silent messages to Kayleigh's heart, which was firmly closed. She turned away again.

Baby gave a tiny sigh, shifted his position, and relaxed into my embrace. I lifted my little finger and gently stroked the tiny face, wiping away his drying tears. A nurse watched through the glass in the door, and pushed it half open. I shook my head. 'Go away,' said Kayleigh rudely. She went. The door opened a moment later and an orderly came in. 'Tea?'

I shook my head again. I'd never felt more like a cup of tea. Kayleigh looked up. 'Nah,' she said dismissively.

'You'll be all right,' I said silently to the sleeping infant. 'You'll be all right, my little one.' I watched his tiny shoulders rise and fall as he slept the sleep of innocence and ignorance.

Kayleigh collapsed on to the pillows; Baby slept. I sat on the bed feeling totally exhausted, yet closer now to Kayleigh than I ever had. Baby could be my grandson. Kayleigh stared at the ceiling.

'What have I fucking done, Mau?' she said finally.

'You've had a baby. You're a mother now.'

'Yeah. I never thought of that.'

I struggled with irritation, how could anyone go through pregnancy without realising that at the end of it you'd be a mother? Who couldn't want to be a mother? I remembered Mothers' Day, that annual reminder of what I had lost, a few weeks ago. It's impossible to ignore or forget Mothers' Day, however much one might want to. Pavements are blocked by huge bouquets of flowers, huge prices, huge blooms, expertly arranged: a minimum of flowers, carefully mingled with greenery to look more. Neither scented nor sentient, their essential emptiness fills the pavements. Where have these monsters come from? They don't look jet-lagged, as real flowers would. They mock us with their size.

One day when the Krew had been mocking Mothers' Day, Kayleigh told the story of how, at infant school she had once made her mother a Mothers' Day card. She had brought it home, slightly sticky, with flowers cut from a gardening catalogue, on the Friday before Mothers' day.

'How sweet,' Mum had said, 'but you should've kept it for Sunday, love. Shall I put it away till then?'

Her mum put it, still in its envelope, on the kitchen shelf. Kayleigh hadn't known what was so special about the card or the day. Next time she saw it, a few days later, it was sticking out from the kitchen bin, which as usual was overflowing. She'd pushed it down into the putrefying mass so that the lid closed with a firm clang. A few days later still, when her mum was forced to empty it into the wheelie bin, the card stood firm, attaching itself to the sides and had to be prised away to liberate the debris lower down. Kayleigh remembered the card, tea stained, weighed down by greasy remains of rejected chips, sighing silently as it sank amid the debris.

Then Shellie told how she had once nicked a bunch of flowers for Mothers' Day, and Mum, at first delighted, then realising they must be nicked, slapped Shellie's face hard. Yet she kept them, and said to a neighbour who happened to come in, 'Look what our Shellie got us for Mothers' Day.'

Now Kayleigh said, 'I just thought of having a little baby girl to love. Now I'm a mum. A mum.'

I stroked her hair. 'It takes a bit of getting used to ...'

'I don't like it.'

Would it have been any different had Baby been a girl?

I spent the rest of the day in the hospital, going to the canteen for rest time. Suze went home eventually, other members of the Krew came briefly, embarrassed, not knowing what to say, not recognising the Kayleigh who lay silent, sulking in the bed. She stopped even looking at Baby; not even the brief glances she had thrown in his direction earlier. Walking home exhausted in the evening, I felt the exclusion Husband must have felt when John and Michael were born. Had I chosen to exclude him, or did he exclude himself? Was this the start of the failure of our marriage? Should I have seen this at the time? How could I, a young mother enchanted with my baby? He sulked. I assumed he was childishly jealous of baby Michael, and tried to pander to his every need, while resenting it more and more.

Kayleigh needed so much support. All she seemed to ask of me was an endless supply of coke.

Exhausted by emotion, I fell asleep as soon as I got home, to be tormented yet again by dreams where John, Michael and Husband in turn accused me of murder or worse.

'I'd still be alive if it weren't for you,' said a strangely real Michael, covered in mud and oil.

'Why d'you think I left?' asked husband, a shadowy figure, with no face. 'You brought it all on yourself.'

'I had to go my own way,' insisted John, dressed in a suit as if for an interview. 'I should have gone years before.'

'You never came to visit,' I said, in tears.

'What was there to come for?'

I wept. 'There, there,' said Gran. 'There, there.' I clutched her, but she vanished leaving me on the ground in the rain. Pain woke me and I found myself with my head banging against the bedroom wall, the blankets on the floor. I picked them up; Worry was hiding inside. What would be the future of this fatherless child? To be brought up by Kayleigh, a mere child herself? To live with me, or to be adopted and brought up by some nice couple desperate for a child, unable to conceive? The hospital seemed to think it would be better for Kayleigh to keep her child. Why? Did they think it was her duty? I had given up all thoughts of duty the day I brought Kayleigh to my home. Or perhaps I had changed my view of duty. Worry had me in thrall once again.

Adoption involved courts, social workers; Kayleigh's parents would undoubtedly have to find out and I would go to prison. It would be a long sentence. Would my age and good intentions count for anything? Kidnapping's serious. Kayleigh was a child. The press would hound me. If I behaved myself I might go to one of those open prisons, said to be like holiday camps. That might not be too bad, but having tasted freedom, I didn't want to be locked up again, this time with a real key. I'd never fancied holiday camps. I tossed about so much I had to get up again to pick up the sheets and blankets.

I lay there, plagued by the heavy weight of Worry, sitting silently on my chest and laughing from time to time in the darkness, telling me I needed Kayleigh to bring Baby home, for my own selfish reasons. 'The hospital want her to keep him, are sure that she will,' I told him. He laughed. 'You want Baby here, don't you?'

Worry mocked me, his grey tentacles enfolding me, paralysing me. I heard the words of a judge in a court, again and again, always the same underlying theme: irresponsible, selfish, exploiting young girls, putting my own needs above the needs of the child. The child floated in and out of my mind, accusing, scowling. Using words Michael, or was it John, or both, had said when angry, 'I never asked to be born.'

'This mess is all your making,' chortled Worry. 'Silly interfering old woman. Witch. You can't replace the family you lost. That was your own fault too. This is all selfishness. You deserve to go to prison. You deserved to lose your family.'

Worry hovered over me, covered me with a dark cloud of helplessness and impossibility. It was 3.30 am. I picked up the blankets once more, and, realising there was no need to be quiet tonight, screamed out in anguish into the black night, but found no comfort.

If Baby were adopted, would Kayleigh still want to live here? Would the Krew continue to make free with my house, now a home once more? I was powerless. I willed away the hours until I could return to the hospital and Kayleigh, in whose hands lay my future. I mustn't try to influence her: it would look bad at the trial.

Might I get off with a suspended sentence? I hadn't meant any harm, but I'd known what I was doing was wrong. Kayleigh's parents would give evidence against me. I'd enticed their daughter away. Persuaded her to keep Baby, when what it needed was adult parents. Why hadn't I thought of all that months ago?

Kayleigh and the Krew would support me, but all their parents would side with the prosecution. They should have known where their daughters had been. They'd never have allowed them to be unpaid painters and decorators, when they should have been doing their homework. Suze's parents would accuse me of encouraging their daughter's inappropriate friendship with Kayleigh.

Those unknown parents would unite to condemn me. There had been months of deception, wilful refusal to realise what I was doing, childish inability to see where my naivety would lead. Would it lead me to the dock? If Kayleigh brought Baby home, there would be more health visitors, social workers, school attendance officers. I could still find myself in prison.

When finally I fell asleep it was to the recurring dream of prison: the echoing landings of so many TV films. Clanging doors, jangling keys of hell, angry footsteps on the long landings.

That dream was worse than the sleepless nights of worry. The first time I had it I woke to screams and shouts, then harsh tinkles of smashing glass, thumps and a flashing yellow light. The early morning rubbish lorry was collecting the street's waste. I lay awake, listening to the crashes. Wheelie bins rumbled along the pavement to be banged finally on the side of the dust cart, as the rubbish of unknown lives was tipped away to nestle with the dirty nappies, rotting fast food containers, and the cans and bottles of those who couldn't be bothered to separate them. Everything was chewed up by the huge jaws of the trundling lorry, with its smell of human failure, rot and faint despair. What incriminating secrets was it carrying off, so that the residents of the street could sleep more easily? Perhaps I should have got myself chewed up with the dirty nappies.

I got up, pulled aside the curtains, watched its slow procession down the street. Dodging the parked cars, the men lifted the wheelie bins effortlessly, expertly, getting vital work done in darkness, at speed. They hurried down the quiet street purposefully unhurried, tipping out the debris, sanitising lives. Papers were snatched from the bins by the wind, and danced down the street, rejoicing in their liberty.

Worry returned, refreshed in the daylight, reminded me that my situation was unchanged. The fast clearing sky showed pink over the roof tops. 'Red sky in the morning,' I muttered, automatically. A dire warning.

Worry had accompanied me through all the decision making, cleaning, ante-natal visits and dental appointments, shopping for Baby and cajoling Kayleigh into accepting the physical side of pregnancy. I had all the answers then; why had I never doubted a happy ending: Kayleigh loving Baby. What had Kayleigh meant when she talked so much about love? She'd never even held a baby, still hadn't. I should have known, did know, that birth is a beginning: parenthood stretches away to the future, should last for ever. The hearse, the coffin, the tall crematorium chimney swam again before my eyes. Michael was finally reduced to ash: motherhood shattered.

Useless tears again wet my eyes as I searched for suitable clothes for hospital visiting. I needed to look respectable, confident, equal to those green uniforms and white coats. I was Kayleigh's aunty. I'd been on the phone to my sister: Kayleigh's mum had a bad cold, but sent her love, couldn't wait to see Baby and would post a card as soon as she felt well enough to go out. I had told her Kayleigh was as well as could be expected, and the six and a half pound boy doing fine, but there were some problems with feeding.

I was slightly shocked at these easy falsehoods. Had I picked it up from the girls or had I always been able to lie like this? Kayleigh's Krew created their lives: if they wanted something to be true, it was. They picked their way through sordid realities, supported by their fantasies, which crashed down on them eventually, leaving them temporarily with reality, which they soon buried once more under a new set of lies. The lottery, promises of love, better times around the corner, all these enabled life to go on. Would my lies last long enough to get Kayleigh and Baby home? They were the wrong lies. I scratched at a patch of spilled food on one of my more respectable jumpers, and peered at it: Aunty Maude couldn't dribble food like a child. I tossed the jumper into the dirty clothes basket and rummaged again in the drawer, picking up a similar jumper and sniffing at it appraisingly. This one had the beginning of a hole in the elbow …

At the hospital Kayleigh was weeping.

'I feels different. He's changed me. I don't like it. Don't want it. Don't want him.'

I looked down at the childish face. How could she not have foreseen this? Why did I not persuade Kayleigh she was too young to be a mother? Told her not to squander her childhood. Baby was now three days old, and there was still no sign of any bonding. I felt the hospital were altogether too laid back about it. Surely they could take some action, not just leave the two in the same room? Could Kayleigh change now? What about three day blues – post-natal depression. Kayleigh was sure to get that. Perhaps that's what was wrong with her? If she was suffering from depression, she would never now accept Baby. What would happen? If she was seriously ill her mother would have to know. I knew what that would mean.

I was in despair; then, when Kayleigh seemed to be falling asleep, suddenly she sat up.

'Help! Me fucking boob's dribbling. They've been feeling horrible. Huge. Horrible hard. They're choking me. What's happening? What can I do?'

I hesitated, 'It's milk for Baby.'

'I knows, I knows. I never fucking knowed it'd feel so ...' She struggled for a word for the hard knot that was tying up her breasts. She touched one cautiously, it was like some unripe fruit, not soft and cuddly as a breast should be. The blue veins stood out, as her blood pumped through these alien beasts, so hard and hot, unyielding and fiery. She was terrified by the power of motherhood, pushing itself into her reluctant body. Milk was calling her, summoned by Baby's cry. It was scary.

'Help, Mau. What can I do? It fucking hurts. Help!'

'Well,' I started, doubtful, 'it's come for Baby.'

Kayleigh was appalled at the thought of Baby drinking her milk, sucking her breasts. She had not thought breast feeding would be like this: her breasts had taken on a life of their own. She looked down in horror: they were as firm as bricks, a few drops of a yellowish something started to ooze through one enlarged nipple. I could see she thought it gross. She twisted on to her front and screamed like a distraught seagull. I could hardly bear this screaming at life, screams were for death.

'It's only milk, colostrum, the very best food for a new born baby,' I said, trying to stay calm.

'Well it's fucking gross. Fucking weird. How can I fucking get rid of it?'

I held my breath. Should I say how much better Kayleigh would feel if she let Baby suck? Then I remembered some, perhaps most, babies didn't recognise a breast when it was first offered them, or know what to do with it. Kayleigh would have no patience with a son who needed teaching. Michael had not found sucking easy, he needed help in directing his tiny mouth to the huge nipple. There he had rooted, snuggled, struggled, but seemed not to know how to suck. How would Kayleigh cope with this? I remembered the frustration, as Michael's instinctive urge seemed out of step with my body's. I remembered Husband's hurt expression as I shouted at his useless words of encouragement; I had thrown a hairbrush at him. Now I was silent, what could I say?

You owe him the best start in life you can, even if you are going to give him away? No. I waited. Kayleigh reached for the tissues, wiping her damp breasts.

'They're so fucking big, and hard, and horrible,' she said, looking down at herself again in horror. She smacked one breast angrily, wincing at the pain, looking down in disgust, as another drop of the thick colostrum seeped from it. I remembered the sensation from years ago, exciting but terrifying, of feeling out of control of my own body. I had surrendered to the urge of motherhood, and relished the basically sexual delight I felt when Michael sucked. Kayleigh had never experienced such delight, perhaps never would, and it was my fault …

I remembered long hours of sitting in the rocking chair feeding first John, a few years later, Michael: feeling the children growing from the love I gave them through my body. A feeling of completeness, of being totally bound to another person. Husband didn't stand a chance. It was hardly surprising that he'd started to grow away from me. That must have been the start.

Baby started to whimper. Kayleigh looked into the cot. She

bent over, her hard breasts hanging damply, and stretched out her arms, but could not reach him. I hesitated. Kayleigh sat up exhausted.

'Give him here,' she mumbled. I hesitated again.

'Fucking give him to me.'

Slowly, I scooped up the tiny angry Baby, his face puckering up for a real cry, and offered him to Kayleigh. I tried desperately to remember which way round would be best. For a second I held Baby to my own breast, tried to see my mirror image, then handed him, gently, uncertainly to his young mother. Any word of warning would be useless.

Kayleigh took the child awkwardly, she was demanding a service from him, not offering him comfort, or meeting his needs. She pulled at her nipple and thrust it at Baby's mouth. I winced. I knew that babies who'd been given a bottle often didn't want to take a breast, it was harder work. I held my breath, surprising myself with a silent prayer: 'Please God, please Baby.' I watched in agony Kayleigh's inexpert handling of her son, her movements jerkily awkward, as if trying to thwart her natural instincts. I struggled not to give advice, not to tell Kayleigh that it would take time, that Baby had to learn.

'Get on with it,' said Kayleigh, angrily, 'you're supposed to be fucking hungry. Well, have summat to eat then.'

Baby seemed to be trying to wriggle away from the nipple, which was standing up pink and proud, like a fairy sandcastle; Kayleigh chased him with her breast in her fist. Milk ran down his face. How long was it before a drop reached his mouth? A tiny tongue appeared. I looked away, unable to bear the suspense. A disgusted sound came from Kayleigh and a whimper from Baby. How long did the struggle between the two young creatures last? A struggle which would end in success for both or mutual failure. Couldn't they see that they were both on the same side? I silently paced the room for what felt like hours.

'Mau?'

'Yes, dear?'

'He won't drink. It's no fucking use.'

Desperately I tried to remember how the nurses had helped me all those years ago; gently I took Baby's head in one hand and Kayleigh's breast in the other and tried to manoeuvre them together. Baby seemed to recognise the touch of an expert, even one half a century out of practice, and allowed the milk to flow into his mouth, and then started, uncertainly, to move his tiny mouth muscles.

I watched mother and son trying to learn the timeless lesson of life from one another. I looked up at Kayleigh, whose stony face showed no emotion, only grim determination. I watched the milk dripping from the other breast, and hoped Kayleigh wouldn't notice.

Would this milk of human kindness not stir Kayleigh's motherliness?

I found myself praying again, this time that none of the

hospital staff would come in and say something bright about the feeding Baby. I could just hear the reply: that would be the end of any chance of reconciliation between mother and Baby. I saw a face peering through the glass: Suze. I held up a warning finger. Suze peered through, crept silently in. Eventually Kayleigh felt Suze's eyes.

'He's just easing me tits a bit, like.'

'Yeah.'

Baby grizzled slightly and lost hold of the nipple. Kayleigh awkwardly tried to put him back in position. 'Try him on the other side,' I suggested uncertainly. This time it was easier, he got the idea more quickly, and returned to his sucking after only a few more expletives from his mother.

'I saw Sam,' said Suze.

'This ain't got nothing to do with Sam.'

'I never said it had.'

'Well then … it's me fucking Baby. He's just taking some of me milk away. Me boobs got so fucking hard. Look at them, they're gross. They hurts and all.'

Baby sucked with increasing confidence, Kayleigh endured it. 'Greedy little fucker, innit?'

Suze nodded. 'What's it feel like?' she asked. Kayleigh was going to a foreign country, from which she would be excluded.

'What?'

'Him sucking you.'

'Dunno. Well weird. Don't like it. Not natural.'

I found it easy not to say, 'What could be more natural?' Baby lost the breast, Kayleigh pushed him away. He lay on the bed, his mouth moving, but not crying.

The door opened slowly, Shellie came in hesitantly. She didn't know what to say

'Lovely little boy, isn't he?' said Suze.

'Boy?'

'Yeah.'

'Oh … what's his name?'

After only a brief pause, Kayleigh said, 'Mark.'

'That's nice, 'said Suze. 'When did you think of that, Kayles?'

'Just now. He's gotta have a name, innit. And I'm the one to give it him.'

'Mark,' said Shellie, considering, as if she had any say in the matter.

'Mark.' Suze searched for an appropriate comment. 'It's just one letter different from Mary.'

'Yeah. Easy to write and all. Not like Suzanne, Kayleigh – all that crap. He looks a bit like a Mark, don't you think, Shel?'

Shellie stared vaguely at the child. 'I got him something,' she said and produced a brown paper packet. Kayleigh decided to ignore it. Suze picked it up. Inside was a tiny crumpled pink dress.

'Pretty,' said Suze.

'I didn't realise he were a boy.'

'Nor me neither,' said Kayleigh. 'He's only tiny. He can wear it. He won' t know.'

'Yeah. Why not? Let's put him in it,'

'Now, Kayles?' asked Suze, sounding doubtful about this. Mark was so tiny, like a doll, but he would resist as a doll wouldn't.

'Why not?'

Kayleigh looked at the little white sleep suit which I had got as a special offer, three for the price of two, wondering how to get it off. As if he were a doll, the three girls managed it, and pulled the little dress over his head. Mark protested, feebly at first, then more loudly.

'Now look what you've fucking gone and done,' said Kayleigh. 'Put him back, Suze.'

Suze gently put the pink clad boy back in his bed; he cried even louder.

'Go to sleep,' said Suze. But Mark's cries became louder, and as angry as only one so small can be. Suze picked him up again, he nuzzled her, still crying. She looked at Kayleigh in despair.

'Give him here,' she said, finally. 'He wants a bit more titty. He's welcome. He ain't got rid of much yet.'

She put him to her breast and there was silence.

Shellie stared in amazement.

'It's what he were fucking howling for.'

A nurse, whom I hadn't met before, looked round the door. We all uselessly willed her to go away.

'You're feeding her,' she remarked unnecessarily and inaccurately.

'It's him not her,' said Shellie.

'Oh,' said the nurse, looking at the pink clad Baby, the blue blanket.

'Mark,' said Kayleigh, more certain this time.

'That's nice,' said the nurse.

'It's his fucking name – Mark.'

The nurse went out again, without ever having really come in.

'What she want?' asked Shellie

'Fuck knows. They're always in and out about summat. Interfering and that.'

As Suze watched Baby sucking, she told me later, she was hoping so hard that Kayleigh would bring this little person home, then she would be able to cuddle him, protect him, as he grew, from the horrors that await all children, especially boys. Surely she must keep him now that he was feeding from her, and had a name?

'Here, I think he's had enough,' Kayleigh said, removing Mark from her nipple;

I can still see it standing out proudly, large. I'm sure Shellie thought it was just like a teat on a baby's bottle.

'Put him away now.' Kayleigh handed Mark to Suze, less awkwardly this time, and Suze held him against her shoulder, as I had done.

'You need to burp him,' she said, rubbing the child's back vigorously. I remember her snort when he deposited his feed on her shoulder.

'What d'you want to do that for?' she asked, putting him back in his cot, rubbing at her jumper with a tissue.

'Ungrateful fucker,' said Kayleigh.

'Just like a baby, innit,' said Shellie, whose dealings with babies were limited to admiring from a safe distance. Suze looked like she wanted to strangle her.

'Yeah, well, whatever.'

Shellie looked into the cot. 'He's sort of bubbling,' she said and picked him up. There was milk all over Mark's face.

'Careful of his head,' shouted Suze, rushing to support it, while Kayleigh turned her back and ignored us all. The other two girls tried to remove the milky substance from Mark and from Suze. By the time Mark was back in his cot, crying only slightly, Kayleigh was pretending to be asleep, perhaps she was trying to analyse what that first breast feed had felt like. I felt she was still desperately unhappy, but perhaps less desperate.

'I'll be off then,' said Shellie.

'Take care,' said Suze, adding, 'Don't tell anyone about this, just the Krew. Tell them it's a boy. We don't want any more pink dresses. Mark,' she added as Shellie struggled with the heavy door.

When Brenda came later that day, she didn't coo, or go 'aah'. She looked at the small form in the pink dress and the blue blanket, then at Kayleigh. She told Kayleigh in no uncertain terms that she should give the baby away, even suggesting that she might find rich parents who might pay for him.

Kayleigh was uncertain. 'Look at me tits,' she said.

'Put them away, they're fucking gross.'

'They're full of milk.'

'All more reason to put them away, innit.'

'He drinks it.'

'So. He can have a bottle. You wants to get yourself out of here, Kayles, think about it,' she said and left.

Poor Kayleigh had been thinking about it for so long. The milk was trickling again. She groaned. Then for the first time picked up her child. He was doing his best for her, but he was only three days old.

This time she allowed herself to watch his sucking mouth, his tiny throat contracting as the milk went down. When she felt relieved she held him over her shoulder as Suze had done. This time he sucked her neck, rooting for more milk.

'That's enough for now, innit,' she said, putting him clumsily back in his cot. He didn't protest.

Yes, it was thirst that did it for Mark and Kayleigh.

* * *

I am so thirsty. If I don't have a drink soon … Could that kill me? Would that be the way to go? So thirsty …

'Hello, love, how are you?'

Is this the kindest voice I've heard so far in this hospital? I look up. It is a minute Indian woman, in a sari, with the first real smile I have met here, using a long pole to dust the top of the curtain rail around my bed. I ought to reply, but my voice doesn't seem to be working. I give a faint nod, and what I hope is a smile. She is being very thorough in her work, as I watch her, carefully moving the cards on other patients' lockers. Mine is bare, apart from my water jug. I make a feeble noise, but she seems to understand, and pours me a glass of water. I struggle to hold it, and she supports me. It's the best water I have ever tasted: given to me by probably the least respected, most poorly paid of those who work here. Yet perhaps the most important, for what is more vital in a hospital than cleanliness? And water?

I don't know any Indians.

* * *

I remember that shop keeper I met when Tiddly disappeared. My search for him was taking me further and further from the safety of home. What was the force that drew me on, refusing to accept the painfully obvious? I wandered through the grey streets determinedly, with no method in my search; I would ignore one invitation from a cheerfully flashing Belisha beacon, and accept the next; perhaps its orange was brighter, its flash faster.

I wandered through the fading back streets where the girls live their lives: streets crowded with narrow redbrick terraced houses, and narrower housing association flats. Here the post office thrived on charging those little yellow keys that feed electricity and gas meters; here third world smells crept up through the gutters. While cars played little part in the lives of most residents, they dominated their streets, parked on both sides, so the bus company had withdrawn its services. The cars preferred to use pavements whenever possible, rather than give way to oncoming traffic, yet sometimes, unexpectedly, they paused and waved pedestrians over. Traffic wardens didn't stray into these streets, even in daylight. Pedestrians crossed the roads at their peril, and were constantly driven off the pavements by the parked cars, which would make a street into an impromptu garage, where men discussed why this vehicle won't go, offering advice, assistance, spare parts from the cars that littered their gardens. The squalor of the Tip was a relief from that of the streets.

On the third morning hunger drove me to the co-op. As its automatic doors welcomed me, I turned back, for my first destination was always the pet food shelves, where I chose carefully from the vast array of cat foods on offer, although Tiddly would demolish whatever I bought. I fled home, and, as I closed the back-door, saw the half-full packet of cat food, a well fed cat looking out at me, rebuking me. Forgetting my hunger, I returned to the search, venturing even further from home. When hunger attacked yet again, I found a grimy corner shop and bought two sticky doughnuts which, I was sure, would taste as if they'd spent too long under their plastic dome. I don't like doughnuts, too sweet, the jam tasteless with sugar, but they were the first things I saw.

'Two of these,' I said to the dark-skinned man behind the counter, who looked at me with suspicion. 'Have you seen a cat?'

'Plenty, lady. Too many cats. What kind of a cat would you be wanting?'

'Black … going grey round his mouth … a white patch on his head, and his tail. Thin.'

'No, sorry,' said the shop keeper, with a smile, and I hurried out, knocking over a box of some strange vegetables I'd never seen before, impatient to be out of that musty smell.

'Your change,' called the man, as the shop bell tinkled; I hurried back took the money, and went to the door again.

'Your cakes,' he called again, and I returned once more. We were both relieved when the shop door finally closed, and I was able give the long suppressed sobs their freedom, taking no notice of the few passers-by, who, after staring carefully, looked away.

I opened the torn paper bag, not quite big enough for the doughnuts, stained red where the jam escaped, and bit into one of the greasy lumps. It tasted worse than I remembered, the sugar over the brown fried crust, with its hint of chips, grated on my teeth. Despite my hunger I threw it down. The second was worse, so I threw that away, then the empty bag. My tears wouldn't allow my 'Puss, puss, puss,' to come from my sugared mouth. I looked around, with no idea of where I was or how I'd got there, needing urgently to be home and wash the sugar away with a cup of tea. I'd been out longer than usual, walked further, perhaps Tiddly had returned in my absence. Where was I? This unfamiliar street could be anywhere. Just as new tears were queuing up behind my eyes, I saw the golden crescent on the mosque winking in the sun above the rooftops. Was that a message of hope? I'd never been happy living so close to it, but I knew my way from there.

The hospital Indian was cleaning. For years I never did any cleaning, didn't see the point when it was only me. But when Kayleigh was coming to see if she wanted to live with me I thought I would tidy up first, before she and Suze came to see the house. Somehow I didn't manage it …

I remember how Kayleigh arrived that afternoon, drenched in the rain. She was alone, and scared; Suze had had parent trouble. She would have been more scared if she had not been so wet. I was scared, though she didn't know it; I think we'd both have been less scared if Suzy had been there. I didn't hear her first knock. I'd got out or the way of hearing my door-knocker. No one had used it for years.

Kayleigh told me later that as she stood under the porch, the house seemed engulfed in damp desolation. She said she was thinking it was empty, when finally a dim light appeared inside, and I opened the door. As she hurried in to escape the rain, she collided with an unstable pile of yellowing free newspapers, which collapsed, making it impossible to shut the door.

'Don't worry,' I said. 'I've been meaning to put these out for months … years.' I kicked at the papers, slammed the door shut. 'Come in.'

Kayleigh followed me into the silence of a gloomy room. Suddenly I could see it with her eyes. Huge dark cobwebs hung in every corner, bulging, like miniature hammocks with sinister invisible occupants. Dust everywhere: its smell doing battle with the smell of cat, both conquered by another smell, more unpleasant than either, which seemed to be in the throat. The light was dimmed by the dust on the light shade. How could she bring her baby here?

'A bit of a mess,' I had said. Mess? Shit-hole Kayleigh would have said. Chaos. Filth. Books all over the floor in collapsing heaps, open pages still waving in the gust from the door. I hadn't touched them for years, or cleaned the threadbare carpet. How could anyone live among so many yellowing books?

I watched her, apologetically. I had not known where to start tidying, so had not started. I saw Kayleigh looking at the books. 'I love books. I used to be a librarian.' A distant, miserable memory. 'I don't read much now, not since ...' unable to finish the sentence.

Kayleigh was shocked. I think she hoped one day to say, 'I haven't read a book since I left school.' That would make sense. How could anyone 'love' books? Perhaps the shiny illustrated kind that her mum probably brought home were OK, bright, interesting, with advertisements, always worth a glance, if not a read. The sort you chucked out when you finished with them. She must be wondering why I didn't do the same.

Books had once been my passion. Seventy years on I can still remember the joy learning to read, the excitement of realising that different letters made up different words – Kellogg's, Cadbury's – and the disappointment when my sons had been less eager to read. Leaving school at sixteen, I had been lucky to see a notice in the local library, where I was a regular customer, saying they needed an assistant. I wanted to go back when the children were at grammar school, but librarians were graduates then, library assistants sixteen.

The silence of the house, no music, no TV, disoriented Kayleigh. Silences on the Tip were different, indoors noise was the norm: if they had no music, giggling filled the space. This was eerie. She told me later that I seemed to be somewhere else. She was about to ask if she could turn on the telly, when she saw the tears on my grey cheeks, filling my wrinkles, like tiny rivers. She needed to get away. Go home. Then she noticed a photograph on the telly of a smiling young man.

'That your feller?' she asked finally, anything to stop the silence.

I started. No one but me, talking to the cats, had spoken in the house for years.

'Feller?' Not a term I recognised. 'My son. My darling. My lovely. My little baby. Michael. Dead.' My tears became noisy.

I could see Kayleigh puzzling about the 'baby': did she picture a cot death perhaps, or meningitis – babies died of that. Or had the baby been crawling in the dust? Could that have killed it? Her baby couldn't live here.

I was in the past, reliving the horror.

'How did it happen?' Kayleigh had to know,

'Motorbike. Death machines. Shouldn't be allowed.'

Did Kayleigh picture a baby under the wheels of a big powerful bike?

'We never wanted him to have it, but he was eighteen. Earning money. What could we do?' The words scarcely audible. 'We said, "take care." What does that mean? How can you take care on a thing like that? He was so vulnerable. "Killed instantly," the policeman said. "Better for him," Husband said. "Better for us. We didn't have to watch him lying in a coma, the life support system blinking and bleeping. We weren't asked if it could be switched off." But I would have liked his life supported at least until I'd said goodbye. It was such a terrible shock.'

Kayleigh had never heard me make such a long speech. I was normally as silent as my house. She said that was when she wondered if she could persuade Suze and perhaps Sam to help her clean up this dreadful place. Perhaps they could spend a day here, get it done. What could they do about that smell? Her mind moved between trying to see the place as it would be when they had finished cleaning it, and my horrific description of the Tragedy.

Kayleigh had once told me that sometimes a teacher tried to explain some stupid poem saying, 'Can you feel what he's trying to say?' She had dismissed this. Not a question anyone could answer. But I could see that she was feeling my pain. Her own eyes were tingling. Perhaps the dust. She put her hands protectively over the developing bulge. Would this still be a baby in eighteen years' time? Longer than her life. I'm sure she wanted to say, 'Maude, I can't bring my baby here. It's hardly better than the Shack. It's dirtier, smellier.' But she couldn't. She shivered. Probably looking for a radiator, but there wasn't one. Just an antique-looking gas fire in an ancient fireplace.

Feeling her chill, I struck a match, and bent down stiffly to light the fire. The smell of gas and sulphur, joined the other smells. The fire's hiss brought some relief from the silence. Kayleigh noticed another photograph, of two small boys, on the mantelpiece.

'Michael?'

I took the frame down lovingly. 'That's Michael', I said, pointing, blowing off the dust, wiping the picture on my sleeve. 'That's John. My babies. Both gone. John could be dead too for all I know. Haven't seen him for years ...' I stopped, back in the past.

John had moved in with his girlfriend some time after Michael's death, I had no idea how long after. 'I'll be in touch,' he said, but he hadn't. I went to the police, who had said there was nothing they could do, he was an adult and it was not a crime to leave home at the age of twenty. His name was added a list of missing people. He sent flowers on Mothers' Day once. A card on my birthday a few times. Christmas cards a bit longer. Never an address, just, 'from John.' Not 'love from ...' That hurt.

For the first few years I had wept when the boys' birthdays came round. On Michael's I used to visit the cemetery where his ashes were buried. Neat lines, serried ranks of small headstones. Obeying orders. Michael would have hated being corralled in this way. Husband and I fought like tigers over what to do with the ashes. He wanted them scattered. But where? On the road? At first I posted cards on John's birthdays addressed to John Bright, and the county, knowing they would be destroyed, unless he worked for the post office. I always signed them 'your loving mother'. Could you love someone you have not seen for years, and did not even know whether they were alive or dead? I loved the memory of Michael, loved the baby, the child, the teenager he had been, despite the fights over the motorbike. He would be a disobedient teenager for eternity. How could I love John? He was no longer a teenager, he was an adult, middle aged. My grandchildren could be adults. Could I even be a great-grandmother? What did they know about me? The tears started again. Anniversaries were things of the past now; I was never sure what month it was, let alone what day.

I spoke again. 'I might be a grandmother. I always thought I'd like that. But if I am, I don't know my grandchildren.

Wouldn't recognise them if I saw them in the street.' Kayleigh grew more uncomfortable, and was appalled, I think, when she heard herself say, 'You could be a Nan to me baby.' I'm sure what she wanted to say was, 'I can't have my baby here in all this dirt and misery.'

She looked at the photos of Michael smiling through the dust, perhaps twenty or thirty of them in dark frames. The early pictures were black and white, changing to colour as the boy grew older: a baby in a long white christening gown held by a smiling young woman; at the seaside, beside a large sand castle, with a smiling man in rather strange shorts; school photos, grammar school blazers. Kayleigh's mum was always too mean to buy school photos. Kayleigh said she used to say, 'I sees you every day. I don't need no photo to tell me what you looks like.'

Kayleigh had learned not to be disappointed. She wondered if she disappeared now, would Mum wish she'd had photos? Would she cry? It might be weeks before she even noticed. She'd be angry more than sad, she'd get over it. Kayleigh's mum wasn't me. I was cleaning another photo on my sleeve, staring at it. It showed four smiling faces in front of a dark blue curtain, two small boys.

'That's me when I was a mother, that's Husband. Ex. Michael. John.' I heard my voice faltering. 'All gone.'

I stopped, back in the past …

Husband had sneaked away, more quietly even than John. I remembered our growing apart, how, after the Tragedy, we slept in the same bed without touching. He'd tried to make physical contact a few times; involuntarily I had jumped away as if a wasp had stung me, the silence and distance grew between us.

* * *

I could do with some silence in here. People coming and going all day and all night, curtains being pulled and pulled back. Orderlies wheeling beds around. No quiet. No peace. Give me back my peace.

* * *

I remember how we tried to tell John of the accident. We did it badly: his face awash with horror and desolation, but above all guilt, at seeing his frequently repeated childhood, 'I wish you were ...' fulfilled. He'd rushed from the house, was gone for some hours and wouldn't say where he'd been.

'We must go on, Maude,' said Husband, 'pick up the pieces. We mustn't allow this tragedy to take over our whole lives.'

'It has. Our lives will never be the same.'

'We've still got each other. John needs us.'

I knew I couldn't comfort him, nor be comforted by anyone, least of all him. Husband and son separated themselves from me, each trying to support the other, putting together a show of normality, that neither of them can have felt.

'Life must go on,' was their mantra; mine, 'Life as I know it is over; nothing can ever be the same.'

'I need to cuddle you, at least,' Husband had pleaded.

'I can't do with tenderness. Not yet.' I wept again.

'For better, for worse,' we had vowed. The worst was so much worse than anything we could have anticipated. From the moment of birth, fear of a child's death is always there for every mother, unacknowledged, but instantly available. When the worst happens, Fear springs out to attack and say, 'Why didn't you acknowledge me? You knew I was a possibility, from the days when you woke him at dead of night, to make sure he was breathing.'

I shrank. Accused. Again.

Husband soon gave up the attempt to include me in the game of pretence, that he and John were playing. Ignored me more and more. Gave up any attempt to even touch me. My Grief thrived on exclusion. Neither father nor brother could begin to understand a mother's Grief. I suffered alone.

Anger, uselessly mingled with Grief, spilled over to those I met accidentally in shops; the old women in the co-op queue, who took so long to find their purses; the weather, when I carried in washing wetter than when I hung it out; people who parked on the pavement; children cycling on pavements. Never far beneath the surface, Anger waited to spring at the least provocation, bringing with him all the 'if only's': if only, if only Michael had listened to me he might be alive today. If only I had pleaded differently, put my terror into words that he could accept; if only I could turn back the clock, rerun those last few years.

With an effort, I finally came back to the present. 'What d'you think? Could we clean this place up enough for you to come and live here?'

Now Kayleigh looked frightened, silent. How could she come and live here? It would take hours, days, weeks, to clean up all the filth. Even if the others helped.

Kayleigh, who once told how her mother complained bitterly and frequently, that she didn't help with the housework, Kayleigh who used to say, 'What's wrong with a bit o' dirt,' now looked at my dirt, unlike any other she had seen, except when Mum had decided to move the fridge a few months ago.

'Give us a hand.'

'It's not my fucking dirt,' Kayleigh had objected, glancing at the greasy filth climbing the wall.

This wasn't her dirt, but she was going to have to give me a hand. She told me later she had secretly watched her mum's occasional, half-hearted wars on dirt, and thought she knew how to do battle. She was starting to plan her campaign.

'It'd need a lot a cleaning,' she said. 'You'd have to chuck some stuff out. New carpet.' She looked up at the ceiling. 'Could do with a coat o' paint.' Did she suddenly see the room transformed, like the houses on the telly on those rubbish programmes her mum liked to watch? Did she think she and I could have a cosy place to live and bring up her baby together? Get rid of that dreadful gas fire? Clean the window? Let in a bit of light.

This new life, unbelievably inside her, was demanding that she do it. Of course she'd love her for eighteen years. Eighty if need be. When her baby was eighty, she'd be over ninety. Lots of people live to a hundred these days.

'What can we do with all them books, Maude?'

I looked around, vaguely.

'They'll have to go.' I wanted to cry again. Only Nazis get rid of books. I might give a few to the RSPCA shop.

Kayleigh left, promising to return next day to start the onslaught, horrified, I'm sure, at what she'd agreed. I felt exhausted, violated. I tried to look at the house with Kayleigh's eyes, see how the spiders had woven their black webs, thick with the dirt and flies of years. I apologised to the house, first for my neglect, then for the coming invasion of its privacy. The house had known worse in its hundred and fifty or more years …

I remembered the day Kayleigh had finally moved in. The Krew all came round to bring her possessions under cover of darkness, one evening when her mum was working at the pub, and her step-dad on the other side of the bar. The duvet had been the most difficult: awkward rather than heavy; anyone meeting her would be sure to say something like, 'Where are you off to, then?' Perhaps they'd offer to help, certainly remember her later, if asked. I'd said there was no need for a duvet, I had blankets. Kayleigh inspected them: scratchily woollen, with a curious smell.

'They're gross, Mau. They stinks.'

'It's only moth-balls,' I said.

'I'll get me duvet here somehow. Nobody uses blankets no more.'

I was used to being nobody. On the evening of the move, I felt like an alien in my own home. Music blasting, back door left open, the house filled with the girls' laughter, swearing, shouting. They'd promised to be quiet, not to be noticed, or draw attention to themselves. I wondered how much noise they made when they were not being quiet.

Kayleigh finally brought the duvet, and banged on the front door with difficulty, as it tried to escape her grasp. I met her, tried to take the duvet, and in the process it fell on the doormat. We both stooped down to pick it up. Heads banged.

'I've got something for you, my dear,' I said. I must have sounded like an excited child waiting to hand over a present at a birthday party. Kayleigh ignored me and dragged her duvet upstairs to John's, her, bedroom. The bed creaked as she dumped it down. I think she told herself this was John's bed, John's room. Could she sleep in the room of a kid who'd topped himself on a bike? She looked out of the window at the lights of the houses in the street behind mine. I looked with her at the view I hadn't seen for years: red brick, all the same, all different, only mine was as it had been for over 100 years. The gardens were very different: some complete wildernesses, filled with dead cars, some lovingly tended, their colours distorted by the street lights. Did she wonder about the people who lived in them: normal people, not like me, not like her. She stood uncertain, and I went downstairs. I called up to her, 'Come down and see what I've got.' She stumbled down. I smiled, and held out the door key to her. She said she'd been meaning to ask for a key, it was a pain always banging the door, the bell broken and me deaf, but now she saw the key in my hand, shiny, newly cut, she hesitated. This was crossing a line.

'You won't have to keep on banging. This is your home now.'

Kayleigh still hesitated. This place home? She took the key carefully, 'Ta, Mau.' I hid my disappointment. I had expected Kayleigh to … what had I expected? That night, amid other troubled dreams, I dreamed she tried to get into the house through the cat flap, but couldn't.

Kayleigh and I each edged warily towards each other for the first few days, each uncertain of what the other expected. Suze called daily, usually with one of the others, to tell her what was going on at school. About a week later they said the police had come to the school and interviewed them all. They told me the unlikely story they had concocted which put the blame on the teachers: Kayleigh was constantly being picked on, said she couldn't stand any more of it. They hinted that she might be in London, but said she might go anywhere where someone offered her a lift. This seemed safer than their first idea which was to refuse to say anything at all. Kayleigh had approved of their story, but told them to bring her mum in for some of the blame: she never listened to her, couldn't care less about her.

I accepted the story. Worry loved it. I had never had to worry about being arrested before. The police seemed to do nothing to find Kayleigh; I think they knew the family well because of Jason. They had done nothing when John disappeared either, so I was not surprised.

It was a long time before Kayleigh confessed that they had made the whole thing up. They'd been worried that I might change my mind after the first few turbulent days, and that Kayleigh's mum might go to the police; so Kayleigh had staged a row with her mother (not difficult) and stormed out saying she was gong to live with Suze's aunt. Kayleigh was fairly sure that her mum would not go to Suze's mum. There had been little previous contact between the two, and that had not been friendly. Did Kayleigh's mum secretly heave a sigh of relief? Had she known her daughter was pregnant? Perhaps this had saved her the trouble of throwing her out, probably to regret it later, but Kayleigh was nearly grown up now. Her mother's life continued almost as it had before. A life of fleeting relationships, of fallings out with partners, neighbours, children. She had told Jason to get out, she might well have been on the point of saying the same to Kayleigh.

Not long after they came with the story that a fuzzy picture of Kayleigh taken from last year's school photo had appeared outside the police station. *'Have you seen this girl?'*

'Don't look a bit like you, Kayles,' Suze said.

Kayleigh went after dark to look at it, and agreed: this was a child, she was now a woman; nevertheless, she decided to dye her hair black. After hearing about that photo I felt I had to buy her the dye for her hair, and I did my best to cut it and give her a home perm.

'Kayles, you look a fright,' said Suze.

'Ta, Suze. Do I look like that picture?'

'You never did. I told you.'

I was woken by Worry that night. What would happen now? It was three in the morning, the blackest, coldest time of night, a time for sleep or suicide. The house creaked and moaned with its own secret life. Was that woodworm on the move, or even deathwatch beetles? Or mice? Or the people next door? What about the roof? The girls and I had cleaned the house, but I knew there were missing tiles, rising damp. I'd neglected it all for years.

I turned over and over, trying to hide from Worry; the blankets finally left the bed, leaving me unprotected from the night's draughts. 'Fuck,' I heard myself say, using Kayleigh's language again. Further sleep was impossible. I found my slippers and went in search of tea. Worry followed me …

When she brought Mark home it was much the same, the days passed in a blur. I almost felt I was living alone again, with Kayleigh and Mark instead of cats. Kayleigh stayed in bed. She showed practically no interest in Mark, other than feeding him whenever he cried, but showing no tenderness. The Krew came and went, cooed over Mark, ignored me. Suze, in particular, cuddled Mark, sang to him, changed him, while Kayleigh lay impassive. If no one else was there Kayleigh called to me to change nappies. I got quite good at it.

The midwife came, and brushed my worries aside. 'She'll come round,' she said.

'Might it be better if the child were adopted?'

'Who can say? Adoption's a lottery. She is feeding him.'

To Kayleigh she said, as she stripped the clothes from the resisting Mark and weighed him, 'He's doing fine. And you're breast feeding. That's splendid. You'd be amazed at the number of mums who can't or won't feed their babies.'

'Who are you calling a mum?'

'Aren't you a mum? You're giving him the very best start in life, that makes you a good mum.'

'I don't give him nothing. He just takes. Me boobs is not me boobs any more. They're his. It's weird. Scary.'

'It's nature, Kayleigh, it's instinct. Our bodies do what they have to do for the next generation.'

'But I can't stop this fucking milk.'

'Why should you want to?'

'Like I said. It's scary. If I was to give him away, I couldn't give them me boobs too, could I? What'd I do?'

'Do you want to give him away?'

'Dunno. That's scary too.'

'Why might you want to give him away?'

There was a long silence. 'I thought he were a girl ...' The words sounded foolish now.

'It's not his fault he's a boy.'

'It's not my fault neither. I can't be doing with boys. He could of warned me he were a boy.'

Kayleigh was getting embarrassed.

'Well, you just carry on feeding him while you decide what's best. You're doing splendidly both of you.' She re-dressed Mark and put him in his Moses basket. As she left the room she said, quietly, more to Mark than to Kayleigh, 'You're a fine young man; I think you'll grow up to be a caring man.'

I'm sure Kayleigh had never heard of oxymoron, but she wondered, as she told me later, much later. Mark would grow up to be a man, that was scary. She searched her memory for men: her dad, dimly remembered, her several step-dads, the dads and step-dads of others in the Krew, teachers. They had all started as tiny babies. They couldn't help being boys. Apparently she and Sue had agreed to bring Mark up to be different, to be a caring man. Was this the start of a unique experiment in child care?

The midwife promised to send her details of a special 'reintegration' unit for pregnant girls to continue their education. She could leave the baby in the crèche, and catch up on her school work. For Kayleigh, reintegration was a bit of a misnomer, she had never been integrated. Managing not to say

119

that leaving school was one of the best things about being pregnant, she contented herself with a pout.

'It won't stay a baby for ever, Kayleigh, you'll need a job. If you leave school now you'll only be able to get cleaning, or work in a supermarket.' Kayleigh had always fancied working at a supermarket checkout. The midwife continued, 'Shelf filling. If you stay at school you could learn computer skills, get an office job, or do childcare and get a job in a nursery, or be a teaching assistant.'

I wondered why she didn't suggest getting A levels and going to university, being a professional. Why did this young midwife, like all those teachers, write Kayleigh off?

Kayleigh was silent. These were not the kinds of jobs she had ever considered when the Krew were fantasising about the day they would leave school. It seemed even more frightening than having a baby.

'Think about it,' said the midwife, writing things in her book, and giving Kayleigh leaflets.

Kayleigh thought of her milk, that mysterious now bluish white thin stuff that Mark was so greedy for, and the way it stirred her whole body as it flowed. She said she hated milk, but if she was to drink it she'd want whole milk, in the blue topped plastic bottles, this stuff seemed even more skimmed than skimmed. Though she wouldn't admit it, I think it was becoming less scary now, in fact almost pleasant, as Mark sucked at it. She got really irate when he sicked it up again. Her milk, on its way to Mark, was trying to drown Doubt. Doubt spluttered, choked, surfaced again. In the contest between Milk and Doubt, surely Milk would win? Doubt would be finally extinguished, his tentacles writhing, his slimy voice silenced.

Kayleigh's breasts knew what her son wanted. 'He wants his titty,' she would say, when I suggested Mark's crying might be wind. She would switch on the television and sit down to feed him.

* * *

Why do they have television in hospitals? There's enough noise without that. Who's watching? Have I the energy to ask for it to be turned down? Who would hear me? Who can be bothered to listen?

'Maude? … Maude? Can you hear me?'

I can, but don't seem able to answer. I try to nod my head, not sure if I've succeeded. Am I being uncooperative? That's what the Krew were called at school, as well as rude and ungovernable. What does that say about the school?

'Where do you live?'

'What day is it?'

'Wednesday, dear.'

'What month is it?' But she seems to have gone again. Why did I ask that? It doesn't matter.

* * *

121

I remember that Wednesday when I took Kayleigh and Suze to my beloved Forest. Mark was a tiny baby, carried in that sling Suze found in a charity shop. It was spring again: time for the long dead world to wake. The chill in the wind seemed different, reminding us of summer's fickle cheerfulness, not winter's threats. The scent of new life blew in the spring clean air. It crawled out of crevices, slippery as a handful of spaghetti, joyful, pouring out uncontrollably where it was not wanted, impossible to put back. Life demanded our attention. The sun rose higher in the sky, the earth moved towards it.

Those days in early spring, when the rising sap told the trees to let their leaves burst out, and the grass to grow, was always the time for the long dead world to wake. How wrong of Babs and her Christian friends to claim that only Christ rose. We all partake of this resurrection. For the first time in years, I was feeling the clutch of the spring.

How had I let all those springs pass me by? Now, once more, I was able to glory in it, feeling the deepest layers of myself coming to the surface, layers long buried, as the ancient mines of tin, copper, coal were buried by Forest trees. I felt I had to share all this with Kayleigh and Mark, pass on the glories of those trees, whose dark shapes were now disappearing under spring leaves. No city plane tree could explode with life like the fresh green beeches of spring. They would soon turn to darker shades, almost dirty before bursting into golden glory in autumn, then hanging, dry and brown, through the winter, reluctant to let go and reveal the trees' essential skeletons, making way for new buds.

In all my days of aloneness I had never returned to the Forest, but held within me memories of its brooding suspicious inhabitants, its picnic scented bracken and the ragged sheep roaming free, by ancient right. I knew it would no longer be my Forest, yet the beech trees, if not the mines, must have survived the commuters and the tourists. Trains once puffed smokily through the Forest trees, carrying away the coal and the wood. Now trains ran for tourists who saw romance in dirt. Once more the power of the beech called me. I studied bus timetables and maps, feeling the Forest beginning to work its magic, melt my doubts. All could be well.

'What for? Sounds dead boring,' said Kayleigh, when I suggested a day out in the Forest. She finally agreed, as long as Suze could come too.

Mark seemed now more and more part of Kayleigh, as he daily established his individuality. He was blossoming with the spring. Was he learning to echo his mother's smiles, or was she learning from him? Watching them together, I realised that Kayleigh had seldom smiled in the past, only giggled. Now, Mark and Kayleigh together were experimenting with smiles. I hadn't smiled for years, couldn't watch TV comedies because laughter hurt. Now, diffidently, I joined in with Kayleigh and Mark, as they tried on smiles.

The day started cold and grey. Suze arrived early and we set off in good time, and so had to wait in the draughty bus station, although our bus was standing locked, waiting for us, the driver reading the paper and smoking in his cab, until past time to leave. Mark whimpered in the cold.

Later, although the sun finally penetrated the cloud, even I had to admit it was not a day for the picnic I had so carefully packed into my long unused rucksack. Kayleigh didn't know that food tasted better outdoors; Suze's family had a barbecue, where Daddy burnt sausages and steaks sometimes if visitors came in summer. Both would have preferred a café. As we sat on the cold rug, where Mark wriggled freely, laughing at the treetops' antics far above him, a cloud threatened rain. We started to pack up, but the sun chased the cloud away with the hint of a fleeting rainbow.

Kayleigh and Suze didn't appreciated the multifarious shades of pale green of the unfolding leaves, or the rounded arch of the young bracken bracing itself to support its delicate fronds, which would shiver gently in the winds of the weeks to come. Nor did they hear the conversations, accompanying the birdsong, between the trees, as their branches reached out to touch one another.

'So many colours, all green.'

'Yeah. Green.'

'Like the biology room.' The girls giggled.

'Was that a cuckoo?' I asked.

'Fuck, Mau, even I can recognise a cuckoo.'

'It's singing cuck but not coo.'

'It's singing "cuckoo". You must be going deaf.'

'Perhaps you need a hearing aid,' said Suze.

'Ear trumpet more like.' Kayleigh giggled, as only Kayleigh could.

'Lots of people in their seventies have hearing aids,' I said.

'You're not seventy, Mau?'

'Seventy five.'

'That's old.'

'I am old.'

'I hadn't noticed.'

Was this is meant as a compliment? With my new bifocal glasses my vision was much clearer. The tops of trees were visible once more: I'd forgotten that delicate tracery, its perfect asymmetrical symmetry brushing the sky. I didn't make so many foolish mistakes, as when a woman in a pink dress walking towards me became a hydrangea hanging over a garden wall as I got closer; or the white bird lying on the pavement which turned out to be a plastic bag. I supposed it was true that we all put our own interpretation on what we see and hear. How I viewed the Krew must be far from how they were seen at school, or at home. Whose was the right interpretation? A hearing aid would bring me still closer to the world most people lived in, but was this the world I wanted to live in?

The most successful part of the day was a visit to a private wood, laid out as a kind of maze, where excavations and spoil heaps from centuries-old mining created a somewhat sinister environment. We walked along a sunken path, tree roots, bare and high above, thrust up from the mossy earth. These roots were so similar to branches. Collecting fire wood in my Forest childhood, I frequently bent to pick up a fallen branch, only to find that it was a surfacing root. Root and branch: which was which? So similar; so different. Roots give us strength.

The girls giggled at the monstrous phallic rocks. A tree clinging on precariously, bearing her breasts to the rocks, teasing them, for they, like her, were rooted to the spot. One day she would collapse, those exposed roots could not hold for ever. Perhaps she would fall on that rock, and her breasts turn to splinters as they met. The sun sifted silently through the dense roof cover, birdsong was muted. The trees grew straight, reaching for the sky. I felt I was in the depths of the earth, like the ancient miners who had created this lunar landscape. Soon the moss gave way to the darker, harder green of ivy, and we found we were looking down at the tree tops. The girls laughed more nervously, half thinking we were lost, as we took a succession of paths leading nowhere. It was too early for carpeting bluebells. Once, at Kayleigh's age, I had lain on that blue, and looked up to the piercing green of the beech trees. I thought: the spring turns the world upside down: green above, blue beneath us. Should we have waited for the bluebells? We could come again later, and again. We must come in the autumn when the beeches burn golden. We could come to the Forest, or anywhere else, whenever we wanted.

A warm sensation of freedom, of being in control of my life washed over me: was this happiness? My heart sang a silent hymn in praise of trees. The girls' giggles subsided into boredom, were they already too old for simple delights? Would springs continue to pass them by?

Later, we walked along a mossy track, as the sun finally fell below the horizon, and the light faded. Here leafless trees shone blackly against the golden orange sky, asserting their rootedness in a world of change. Day began to give way to night, but the trees knew that night would yield in her time, as the sun reclaimed the sky. Night into day, day into night. The trees had seen it all before, every day for hundreds of years. I gloried in it, finding words inadequate to express my feelings. Kayleigh's indifferent acceptance was probably closer to the attitude of the trees.

To the left a nearly full moon was rising as the blinding sun sank to the right. The moon lit the intricate lace of twigs, which was lost in the sun's glaring light. Another world spoke at night, a world of mystery, of different realities, different shadows.

'Just look, it's too beautiful for words. Can you feel it?' I could not resist saying.

'Dunno,' said Kayleigh. 'It's pretty, but it's dazzling … How much further?'

'Not far. I feel as if I could walk for ever.'

'Well I don't. Mark's whinging. I could do with some tea.'

'Shall I take him for a bit?' I liked carrying Mark, but he was getting heavy and I was glad when Kayleigh said, 'Nah, that'd wake him up proper, then he'd want me tits again, and we'd never get home.'

'You could sit on that tree trunk for one last Forest feed.'

'I'd rather be home in the warm. With a cushion and a cuppa.'

'There's a café in the village. We'll have time for a cuppa waiting for the bus.'

We sat in the grimy café drinking hot chocolate and tea, the steam rising from our cups to join the greasy smell of chips and the friendly roar of the coffee machine, bubbling like a mini volcano. Escaping to this human fog, from the cold of the approaching night, we all felt content. Kayleigh fed Mark. I was both touched and slightly nervous at Kayleigh's careless openness. She never tried to be discrete, almost flaunting her breasts, as if hoping that someone would object so that she could defend her right to feed her child in public. I thought I could see looks of distaste from a table occupied by a young couple, holding hands and gazing at each other. Maybe there was something in Kayleigh's attitude that made them keep their objections to themselves. To Kayleigh breast feeding was as natural as shoplifting.

Kayleigh handed Mark to Suze, finished her chocolate quickly, and took him to the ladies, returning almost immediately.

'There's no baby changing facilities here,' she said to the grim man behind the counter.

'We don't normally get babies.'

'Well we wouldn't have fucking come had we known. You're probably losing a lot of trade.'

'I doubt it.' He turned to his next customer. Kayleigh pushed the cups to one side and laid Mark on the table. The proprietor watched, opened the flap of the counter, thought better of it, and returned to his customer.

'Won't be coming here again,' said Kayleigh loudly as we left the café.

This time I was sure I could hear the words, 'Thank goodness.'

At the bus stop an elderly couple, his face a walnut, hers hidden behind a royal headscarf, held hands from which blue rivers rose and mingled. After the mandatory cooing over Mark, the old man said, 'Been having a day out in the Forest, then?'

'It's so lovely at this time of the year,' I said.

'Ah. Seen any wild boar then?'

'What's a wild boar?' asked Suze.

'Like a pig?' I suggested.

'Nah,' said the old man. 'They're huge, bristly, with great big fangs. They've been known to attack people. Could kill a grown man. They used to live wild in the Forest hundreds of years back. But they all got eaten. Farmers keep 'em nowadays, they're served in posh restaurants, but some escape and roam wild, looking for food. They'd eat anything they would. That's why they're so tasty – better than pork any day.'

'Maude!' said Kayleigh. 'How could you let us walk in them woods knowing we might be gobbled up by fucking wild bears.' Was the girls' terror real?

'Boar, not bears. I've never heard of wild boar in the Forest. I'm not sure I believe it.'

'It's true enough,' said the man. 'There's a notice in the car park telling people to keep their dogs under control, some have been attacked.'

'There you are, dogs. Not people.'

'They could though.'

I cursed the couple, who settled themselves downstairs when the bus came, so I led the girls to the top deck. Would they ever venture into the countryside again?

I sank exhausted into my seat, looking out of the window, watching the last streaks of the dying light fading. I gave thanks, to whom or to what I was still not sure, for these girls who gave me back my life. Whatever happens, nothing could change that last year. Despite everything, I had lived. There must be some power to be thanked. Is that why man created god, as I read somewhere, because of a deep need to give thanks? Do we all create our own individual gods? Mine was not a god who grants wishes: what would I wish for? I remembered the fairy story about sausages on a nose. I gave thanks to my cloudy Forest Goddess that the rain held off, for neither girl had adequate waterproofs, and despite my advice, neither wore sensible shoes.

I closed my eyes and thought about the day. I was at first

disappointed that the girls didn't want to walk far; they walk to get somewhere not for pleasure. I suspected that Kayleigh would never want to walk further than the corner shops for cigarettes. This had been a short walk, but I was nearly tired. Ten mile walks were things of the past now: the long buried dream of The Moor or the Scottish mountains would never now come true.

In the seat behind me, the two girls were talking seriously, their giggles muted, laughing quietly from time to time. Mark slept in his mother's arms. It was dark now, the view of the trees hidden, as was the ugliness of the sprawling mining villages.

I drifted into that hinterland between sleep and waking where dreams mingle with reality. That morning I'd looked in the mirror again. The grey face that looked back at me returned now blackly in the bus window, as I approached sleep. Deep shadows filled the wrinkles.

'Grey is the colour of life,' said the face. 'Grey is reality; the colour of mountains, their yin and yang woven to a grey which speaks of their power, and their danger. Lower mountain slopes are lush, green with grass and moss, flowers thrusting though. As we climb higher, green gives way to grey. First grey patches in the green, then small patches of green showing through the grey of the stone. At the summit only grim, grey reality. The ground is hard. Legs ache. The path grows steeper. Look around: all is grey ridges, this is why we climb. Grey is greater than green.

'Look closely, in the crevices the grey rocks sparkle with all the colours there are. As we near life's end we grey. We must learn to love the grey, to rejoice in it.'

But grey is the colour of my gremlins, Worry, Grief, Confusion ... Grief and Worry were still lying in wait, ready to snatch my contentment. I feared Confusion. But why did I see them as grey? 'They're colourless,' said the face, 'invisible. Unreal. Grey is the power of the mountain.'

'Have faith,' Babs had said. 'If you have faith you can remove mountains.' Who would want to remove a mountain? I drifted gently on a comfortable cloud of acceptance. All could be well.

Kayleigh and Suze must have thought I was asleep, and couldn't hear them discussing in such a controlled and adult way: should Kayleigh take Mark to visit her mum, perhaps even move back there, if her step-dad had left? I listened, horrified, were they going to snatch away the nearest approach to happiness I had allowed myself for years? But I was compelled to give myself up to sleep, only waking as the bus bumped into the draughty bus station.

I heard Kayleigh say gently, 'Don't she look small, Suze?'

'Tiny, Kay.'

'If we left her here, no one might notice her.'

'We can't leave her in the bus all night.'

Mark woke with the stillness of the bus, and the silence; Kayleigh rocked him in his sling, 'Hush, Mark love, I'll feed you when we gets home.' She raised her voice. 'Come on now, Mau, love, if you don't want to spend the night in the depot.'

I opened my eyes. Did I really hear Kay thinking of going back to her mum? Mark's thin cry of protest at the cold night air blowing up the stairs brought reality back. I gradually unwound my stiff body from the unnatural shape the bus had forced it into.

Kay never said any more about going back to Mum, so perhaps I dreamt it …

That day winter had struggled with the spring. I remembered another day shortly after Kayleigh moved in, after a cold, wet, dark November, which dawdled into a darker December, the weather became so spring-like that it was impossible to believe it was nearly Christmas. Spring in December. Nothing was impossible. Life would return to a long dead world.

Looking at the weeds covering the tiny front garden, I had noticed a flash of pink that had not been there yesterday; a primrose, or primula, had forced its way up through the hard earth towards the sun. Next day another even paler pink flower appeared. I had no idea what this one was, its delicate petals clustered together as if for comfort, I saw it tremble as I approached. Gran must have planted these and they had survived, quietly blooming each spring, ready now to show themselves, to shame me for not having seen them for so long. I remembered the garden in Gran's day, pink scented roses, Gran's delight; the back garden was Granddad's territory, where lettuces and cabbages stood to attention and the feathery green of carrots waved to the golden onion domes. From time to time loads of horse manure would be delivered, and the neighbours complained approvingly of the life-giving country smell. I had tried to follow Gran's example, but never quite achieved it. Husband took over granddad's patch; he was of a different generation, so fertilisers and weed killer, rather than manure and the work with a hoe; the rows were less straight, the weeds less speedily dispatched. I felt a gentle nudge from Guilt. 'You could have tried again, once you had it to yourself.'

Now, as the sun played games with the seasons, I went purposefully to the garden shed. The tools still hung neatly in their ranks on rusting nails: spade, fork, rake, hoe, then higher up trowel and miniature fork. These last I carried through the house and tried to dig out the weeds clutching at the primroses. But the weeds were less fragile, their roots stuck firm in the ground, determined to keep the territory they had invaded. I gave up when I accidentally knocked off one of the flower heads.

'I'm so sorry,' I said. 'I'm not good at this.'

I held the petals in my hand; they looked up at me, reproachfully, trembling. 'Leave us alone. We can cope. We don't need you.'

I returned the tools to the shed, but couldn't make them hang where I'd found them. They clattered off their nails twice before I left them carelessly on the bench, where they, too, seemed to reproach me for not knowing how it was done. I glanced at the lawn mower, would it still work? Could I use it? I turned away. The house was all I could cope with at the moment. The garden would have to wait.

Inside, the low winter sun lit up the sitting room, though hindered by the smudges and streaks on the glass, memories of the redecoration, a few weeks ago now. I rummaged in the kitchen drawer for a cloth. Window cleaning was my territory. If I couldn't help the flowers on their sunward journey, at least I could ease the passage of the sunlight. Vinegar, I remembered, was good for windows. I found a dusty bottle, its cap rusted on. With memories of fish and chip suppers, I carefully added some to a bowl of warm water, carried out a chair, and balancing precariously on it, started work, the acrid scent rising to my nostrils with the steam. The small Victorian window was taller than I remembered, I stretched. The ground was not as hard as it seemed, and yielded to the weight of the chair, which tipped dangerously lopsided. I came down, the vinegar water splashing my slippered feet, righted the chair and climbed up again.

'Hi, Mau. What you up to?' Suze and Kayleigh came into the garden. With difficulty I again came down from my chair. This time the bowl slipped from my hands, soaking my slippers, and making a small patch of pickled mud on what had once been the lawn.

'Hello. What a lovely day. The sun was making the window look dirty, but it's not as easy as it was.'

'Can we give you a hand?' asked Kayleigh, in tones that clearly expected the answer, 'No.'

'You can put the kettle on. I'll have another try later.'

Kayleigh and Suze escaped to the kitchen, and while Kayleigh filled the kettle, Suze searched the cupboards for biscuits.

I took off my wet slippers, settled into the armchair, and watched the dust perform its dance of hope in the filtered sunlight, listening to the girls laughing and chattering. I relaxed slowly, soaking up the sun's healing rays, which showed up the smudges and missed patches of the girls' inexpert painting. How Husband would have tut-tutted over their careless work. He would have gone to the shed for a brush to do it over again. I could live with it.

'Thanks, love.' I took the mug of warm, rather too weak, rather too sweet tea, as Suze offered the biscuit tin, once again nearly empty. I watched a biscuit disintegrate as I dipped it rather too long, then sucked at the soggy mess.

'You're good girls. I needed that.'

'You and your tea, Mau.' But I noticed that Kayleigh was also drinking tea this time – was it a pregnant craving? – while Suze had a glass of squash, and a handful of biscuits.

I managed not to say, 'You'll spoil your dinner,' or 'You'll never lose weight that way.' Words from another life. I swallowed them with the weak tea. Again I resisted asking Kayleigh to leave the tea bag in just a bit longer. The sun lit up a threadbare patch in the charity shop carpet, and its accumulated fluff that came from nowhere. I relaxed more deeply into the power of the sun, remembering how in the past this would have had me jumping up to take action. I could move the sofa a bit to cover the hole in the carpet. I thought vaguely that I was beginning to darn the hole in my life.

'The days will soon be getting longer,' I said, remembering Husband's winter depressions, his need to be reminded when the worst was over.

'Day's twenty four hours, Mau.'

'Yes, but in winter most of those hours are darkness. We'll pass the darkest day in a couple of weeks, and then there'll be more daylight.'

Kayleigh didn't think in seasons. Sometimes it was light, sometimes dark. If asked, she would have said the dark was winter, but it wasn't something to remark on. So she didn't.

'That's why we celebrate Christ's birth as the days get longer.'

'That were December 25th.' Kayleigh knew some things.

'Probably not, it was probably in the summer. There was already a mid-winter festival, so the early Christians decided to add Jesus' birth to that.'

'In the bleak mid winter.'

'It may have been bleak, but there was no snow in the Holy Land. Hot and dry.'

'Mau, you do have some crazy notions … Mary'll love Christmas next year. She'll like all them pretty lights and all.'

'She'll be nine months old. Old enough to know something

special's going on. Not old enough to understand.' I remembered the growing understanding of Christmas in the boys: each Christmas a year older, more fun, more work. I remembered John telling Michael there was no Father Christmas. Michael was bitterly disappointed. I was cross with John, who said he'd tried to keep it to himself when he discovered, so as not to upset Michael, but now the time had come for honesty. 'I think it's wrong to lie to children,' said seven year old John.

As Christmas approached the girls became wilder, noisier. Was the season inevitably rubbing their noses in their families' exclusion from so much of the festivity? I wondered what family Christmas would be like for the Krew: drunkenness, certainly, disappointment with gifts and food that had been impossible bargains? Rows? Violence? Could I help them to get through it? I gritted my teeth. A few days ago Kayleigh had come in with Suze, and started to hang pink tinsel all over the house: a pathetic attempt to appear normal, just like everyone else?

I remembered that dreadful first Christmas after the Tragedy. Husband trying to do everything as we always had, John trying to follow his father, me wanting nothing to do with all this going through the motions. I watched the frantic buying, the queues in the shops, the lights, the drunken parties: were they all attempts to hide the emptiness of life? Perhaps we were not the only ones going through the motions. There had been no decorations in the house since then, certainly no pink tinsel. Tinsel is sliver.

The girls were spending longer and longer at my house; could being able to come here help them to get through what was just another day to be got through? You can't forget it's Christmas, not if you watch television, or go into shops. For the first time since Michael's death I realised, from a television programme, that I was not alone, or unique, in my grief. Children, babies even, die all the time. I was just one of an army of mourning parents, for whom life, and Christmas, would never be the same. A huge nameless multitude, which I had never before considered. Each one shut away from all the rest to bear their pain alone. Christmas meant birth. Hope. A new beginning. Blessedness. But crucifixion followed nativity. For some, hope died almost at birth. I renewed my determination that this must not happen to Kayleigh's child ...

The year of the Tragedy we received fewer cards. Babs, however, chose one with the words 'Merry Xmas', the inside filled with her primary school teacher's handwriting telling us that we would get through the festive season more easily if we could accept that Jesus had come to save us.

I had tried to screw it up and throw it in the bin, but the thick card cut into my hands. I tore it into tiny pieces, and flushed them down the loo. I'd sent no cards since then, but this year I sent one to Babs in response to her usual pious wishes. It showed a drunken Santa, wishing her a sparkling Christmas. I smirked quietly, and wrote: 'You'll be surprised to hear from me. My life has taken a surprising turn, and I am well.' After some thought I added, 'Give my love to Paul and the family. Maude.'

I put the card from the local church, but not Babs', on the mantelpiece among Kayleigh's garish collection from the Krew. I would never celebrate the birth of Babs' Christ, bringing sin and blood. Love came down at Christmas. Love and light: light shining in darkness.

That year the meaning of Christmas seemed to reproach me for my years of neglect. Which year was it? Time plays tricks on me. Time doesn't heal. Christmas was a time of hope: a baby in a manger. Had I changed the story? Found room for Kayleigh in my inn?

Watching her swelling body, I felt the need to celebrate the coming child, for every child is a Christ child: a child of God. I needed to pray that all could be well, light would prevail. I started to cook, digging out ancient recipes, leaving pudding mixture overnight before boiling it.

A few days before Christmas carol singers moved into my head. At first I worried, then Worry moved out temporarily. It was quite different from the common-or-garden tune on the brain. These, I thought, came from the choir of King's College Cambridge, whose service on the Home Service, now Radio Four, had been the start of Christmas when I was a child. They sang beautifully, my body echoed to the organ's booming, the notes rose to the high fluted ceiling with its delicate tracery, looking so much like winter trees. The words were clear, and comfortingly meaningless:

'Hail the incarnate deity.'

'Veiled in flesh.'

'To save us all from Satan's power'

'Born that man no more may die.' What about women? In the whole Christmas story Mary is the only woman.

The carol singers in my head reminded me of nativity plays; kings came from lands afar, Jesus was rocked away in many mangers, shepherds watched. The boys had been in nativity plays, when their voices were like some of those singing to me now. One day I stood outside a chapel advertising a nativity play. If I had been a Gran I could have gone officially, not crept in, hoping no one would notice me. I braved it. Perhaps one of my unknown grandchildren would play a part, Joseph, perhaps or the angel Gabriel. But Gabriel seemed to be played by a beautiful little blue-eyed girl. Why the sex change? I watched the little girl playing Mary, so sweet, so innocent. The virgin Mary had probably been around Kayleigh's age. At least in this day and age, Kayleigh did not need to be married off to anyone who would have her with her child, or have it adopted, as had happened to one of my friends, who had been persuaded to give her son away when he was six weeks old and had never seen him again.

Perhaps there were some things worse even than losing sons at twenty; at least I had seen mine grow to be almost men. Some things change for the better. The familiar tears warmed my eyes as *Away in a Manger* was sung. Husband would have said, 'Pure sentimentality.' It was pure.

'Where've you been?' asked Kayleigh, when I returned home. 'I'd have come too,' she said, slightly petulantly when I told her.

'I didn't know I was going. It was a spur of the moment thing. I didn't think you'd be interested.'

'I were in a nativity play once, when I were an infant.'

'I expect your mum was proud of you.'

'She didn't bother coming. I were an angel.' She laughed at the idea. I caught a hint of regret in the laugh, and sank back into nostalgic memories of Christmases past.

The girls bought cheap gifts for each other, but did not wait for the great day to open them. Kayleigh even found a card for her mum, a glitzy nativity scene, with Mary looking particularly insipid, holding the baby as if she had no idea what to do with it.

'What'll I write, Mau?'

'Tell her you're OK.'

'Am I?'

'Aren't you?'

'Dunno.'

Kayleigh wrote carefully and slowly, 'To Mum. Hope you are OK. I am. Don't worry. See you soon. Love Kayleigh.'

'That's nice, Kayleigh,' I said, wondering about the 'love' and the 'see you soon'.

The girls brought Kayleigh cards from school. She opened them cautiously.

'You told them where I were!' she exploded, on opening an

obscene computer generated card from Daryl, who had sent them to all the girls he'd had sex with.

'No. I haven't told anyone,' said Suze. 'We said we'd met an aunty of yours who knew where you were, and said that you're OK, said she'd deliver the cards.'

'What aunty?'

'We made her up.'

'I don't want me mum finding where I am. What would happen then?'

'I'd probably go to prison,' I said, and wished I hadn't.

Suze thought about it. 'Mau, did you think you could be put in prison when you said Kayleigh could come?'

'I realised it was possible, yes.'

Kayleigh and Suze looked at me. Some of what fun there was seemed to go out of Christmas …

On Christmas morning the choir in my head changed, this time accompanied by a full orchestra: *Glory to God in the highest … and peace on earth*. It was Handel's Messiah, and that must be massed cathedral choirs. I could hear the music rise to an ancient roof, past those strange mediaeval carvings. Then the wonderful solo, which should have preceded the chorus: *There were shepherds abiding in the fields* … I was glad that this year I had at least made an effort to join the worship. The next day I was back in King's College, *Adam lay ybounden* … Women taking the blame for men had a long history.

On Christmas evening, the whole Krew came, sitting round

my gas fire drinking my coke, eating my mince pies. I was sure that it was only because of Kayleigh that they were not smoking or drinking alcohol. They giggled, a slightly different giggle, a Christmas giggle. They knew Christmas was Humbug, a humbug from which they were excluded. Once again outside, looking in. They had no choice but to ridicule it. I looked round at their faces, children's faces, troubled lives carefully concealed beneath the careless show of uncaring: who needs a family? Their alienation protected them.

Christmas – the season when the unspeakable could be spoken, the unforgivable inadvertently confessed, the inadequacies of relationships illuminated in the glaring lights. A time when it was more difficult than ever to play at happy families. The worst things in my life seemed to have happened at Christmas. Mother's TB had been finally diagnosed on Christmas Eve; the Tragedy had been a couple of months before Christmas; Husband had left a week before Christmas; Gran died on boxing day. The season of light in the darkest days illuminated much that should have been allowed to remain in the shadows. Not a safe season, not cosy. Whenever I overheard people talking about it afterwards, however, I would hear, time after time, 'How was your Christmas, then?'

'Lovely.' Always lovely. Christmas is, must be, lovely, however disastrous.

For most of the Krew, such Christmas disasters happened all the year round, on a regular basis, had all happened long ago, pretences were no longer there to be destroyed. Yet I sensed their desperation, more exposed than usual, their giggles ratcheted up a few decibels.

The girls were now my family. I looked at each face in turn, lit by the dreadful flashing lights that Kayleigh had insisted on my buying: would she cope with motherhood? What would happen to the others as they became adults in an uncaring world?

Between Christmas and the New Year the carol singers moved out of my head as inexplicably as they had arrived, to be replaced by Worry, who grew more and more troublesome as the birth approached.

After Christmas, the year stretched ahead, only a few more months until the birth of the baby. As the days lengthened, in that dead segment of the year between Christmas and Easter when resolutions break, flu lays waste, bad weather and strikes disrupt carefully laid plans, the Krew drifted back to the Tip. Suze would call for Kayleigh, whose struggles to get through the hole in the fence grew daily. She needed to be away from me.

Left alone, I appreciated the peace and quiet, but with a slight regret that the Tip's magic was no longer for me.

Winter eventually passed, its cold giving way grudgingly to a reluctant spring. The sun shone, but did not warm. Kayleigh and I settled into a waiting existence, wary of each other, our lives balanced precariously. Kayleigh celebrated her fifteenth birthday quietly, with a cake and candles. The presents were all for the baby, Kayleigh did not show that she cared: an early taste of motherhood. I remembered my boys' birthdays, somewhat guiltily. Kayleigh said her mum often forgot her birthday altogether.

As Kayleigh's pregnancy moved into its last few weeks, she slept even more, visited the Tip less; the Krew came to see her less frequently, sensing that she was leaving them behind, moving into the mysterious, murky world of motherhood …

Finally Kayleigh told me the truth about the baby's father. First she had told the Krew it was rape. No one believed her lurid story. Eventually she answered my question, 'What really happened?'

'It were Daryl.'

She told me how she bumped into Daryl one day, when they were both skiving off maths. Daryl had looked at her, said something pleasant, she couldn't remember what, she had giggled, and to her surprise, had let him put his arm round her and kiss her. Even more to her surprise she had not kicked him. She returned the kiss, and let him lead her out of the school to the teachers' car park. There, behind the mini buses, 'He fucked me. I fucking let him. Dunno why. Never fucking thought about it after, till I realised I were preg.' She paused. 'I'm glad I did though, Mau. Glad I'm having this baby. But she's fucking mine. Not Daryl's.'

'Thank you, Kayleigh. I appreciate your honesty,' I said.

* * *

This thirst will kill me. But not gently.

   'Cup of tea? … I said, cup of tea, Granny?'

   'Yes, please, a cup of tea would be lovely. Milk, no sugar.' My voice seems to be working.

* * *

I remember asking the Krew that very question when they came to help clean up the house before Kayleigh moved in. I remember the chaos, the turmoil. I looked round my sitting room: furniture piled up in the middle, books on the move, dust flying like November-the-fifth smoke. Some books were waiting to go to a charity shop, some piled on the table awaiting a decision on their fate; my most precious I had carried upstairs to my bedroom, where they replaced the piles of dirty clothes. I was trying to re-connect with the world of books: which were the ones I could not bear to be parted from? Would they still mean to me what they once had? Kayleigh was becoming impatient. She wanted to get rid of the books, why couldn't I make up my mind? I managed to be firm: I had to think. I watched the Krew's unlikely enthusiasm helplessly. What had I done? I should never have invited Kayleigh. This was all so different from the satisfying feeling I used to experience when removing dirt in the old days, when this house had been a home. Then, when a mother, I had cleaned it daily, shouted at the boys to, 'Pick it up and put it away,' or 'Shut that door, don't let the heat out.' It had been cosy then. In the evenings, when all was quiet, I relaxed into the contentment of motherhood. My days were filled with meaning and purpose. I thought young girls these days have babies, put dummies in their mouths so that they can't cry, can't laugh, put them in nurseries, and go to work as soon as they can. They missed the joys of motherhood: that magic of being part of another's life, part of creation, watching a life unfold and become itself.

I had made some effort to clear away a bit of dirt before the girls, whom Kayleigh had dragooned into helping, arrived. I had looked at those huge cobwebs, bulging with their tiny malignant ghosts, fetched a broom and brushed them off, bent down to remove the strangely sticky remains from the broom. As I opened the lid of the kitchen bin the stench of decay rose up, accusing me. I took it outside and tipped it into the wheelie bin, which was even smellier. Was it something dead? Tiddly could not have got in there, could he? I closed the lid quickly. The kitchen bin still stank; peering in I saw something sticking to the bottom that had refused to move. I banged on the side of the bin, but it still stuck, hanging on tenaciously. I found a stick, and finally dislodged it, half of it fell on the path, I had no idea what the green fringed mess could be, as I shovelled it up into the wheelie bin.

When would the men come to remove this smelly detritus? Better be rid of it as soon as possible. I manoeuvred the unwieldy bin carefully to the alley, making a faint track on the dewy grass, and out to the pavement, where any passing stranger could, if they wished, smell my life.

Then I realised I needed the bin for the rest of the rubbish. There was little room in it, but better than nothing; I pushed and pulled, and finally dragged it back over the grass, where it made another little pathway of indecision. I heard Husband say, in the days when we went walking, 'The best trod paths are those that lead nowhere, everyone walks them twice.' There was a hint of the triumph of having an original idea in his voice. 'Go away,' I told him, 'you don't belong here. I'm free now to choose my own path.'

Suze, Brenda, Tiger, Kat and Kayleigh were now painting the sitting room walls, having first washed them with an energy that surprised me; I had never seen them physically active before. They usually moved slowly, languidly, as if they were above such things as bodily exertion. They had dressed in old clothes, mostly out-grown, which showed that they were no longer children. There were really too many helpers for such a small house. The paint was going everywhere, the girls laughing at it, not quite daring to throw it over each other. I was sure they'd never done anything like this before. Tiger's anger was scrubbing away at the dirt on the worn window sills.

The ancient furniture, handed on to me by Gran, who had acquired it from her mum, had been waiting patiently for this. At first the girls had mocked the dark wood, but nevertheless had carefully wiped it, then polished it with some modern potion in a plastic spray bottle, which Sam filched from her foster mother.

'Come up lovely,' said Suze, unaware of sounding just like Mummy. When they decided on painting, the furniture was swathed in layers of old newspaper, which blew away each time a door was opened. Feeling somewhat superfluous in all the unlikely activity, I made myself responsible for picking up and replacing the paper.

Kayleigh had brought her music system, and it was blasting us all with the kinds of music I normally avoided, hurrying past stationary cars and other places where it was played. It was raucous, with a heavy beat. I realised in horror, that from now on such music would fill my home. I had not thought of that when I made my offer. There were so many things I had not thought of, did not yet know about, did not want to think about, which appalled me. Somehow I would have to learn to live with this; it was quite like Michael's music. Husband had shouted at him, 'So long as you live in MY house ...' I could hear him so clearly. I didn't bother to contradict him. I'd invited Kayleigh, this was to be her home, she had the right to her music. My slight deafness might help, so I said nothing, not even, 'Could you please turn it down a bit?' That might come later.

Suze discovered the heavy wooden radiogram, which had been a wedding present. The Krew watched as I played one of my 78 records, still in the cupboard that was part of the machine. I explained that you could load it up with several records, and it changed them automatically. I remembered marvelling at the clunk, as each one dropped on to the turntable.

'It's like a museum here,' said Suze. The rest of the Krew only visited museums on school trips, they were boring. Yet they seemed to look at me with some kind of respect; I was old, really old, I came from another country. Weird.

'I used to live here with my Gran and Granddad when I was a child,' I said, beginning to enjoy myself. 'Gran had a wind up gramophone, and an old wireless that needed an accumulator.' I remembered carrying the heavy glass object to the garage around the corner to be recharged. I told them how I had to be very careful not to spill the acid that swirled between the metal plates.

'No electricity?' Kayleigh could not imagine a world without switches.

'Nor gas.'

'How did you cook?'

I recalled the oil stoves, perched on a stone slab in the kitchen, and the greedy, black range, lit, with difficulty, on baking days. It was another world. The girls began asking questions. I told them of waking up on winter mornings to see ice on the inside of the window. They shivered as I remembered the fragile, frosty leaf patterns, which only melted if the sun moved round.

'On the insides of the windows?'

'We wore bed socks. Granddad put bricks in the oven, which Gran wrapped up in bits of old blanket – to use as hot water bottles. There was no rubber in the war, it was all used to make aeroplane tyres.'

I marvelled at the gulf between my childhood and theirs. It became some kind of bond between us. I hummed the signature tune of *Music while you Work* on the wireless, remembering Digging for Victory and Granddad's stories of First World War trenches. They tried to explain mobile phones, texting, computer games.

In my childhood rebellion was forbidden; parents were obeyed, feared. I had been brought up to do as I was told, these girls seemed hardly to have been brought up at all. They swore, shoplifted, bunked off school. But they cared for one another, as I don't remember caring for my friends. I watched them work, breaking carefully painted fingernails, splashing paint on their faces. Would all this turn my house back into a home?

Suze had suggested using the vacuum cleaner, and I finally found it in the old scullery. Suze turned out to know a lot about vacuum cleaners. 'Needs a new bag,' she said, when it seemed to be puffing out dirt rather than absorbing it. I found a bag, but then the machine made a dreadful noise filling the house with the smell of burning rubber. Suze turned it upside-down. 'Needs a new belt,' she diagnosed. She also knew where to buy one.

I have always found it hard to spend money. When I offered

a home to Kayleigh one of my first thoughts had been could I afford to keep her? I went to that still slightly alarming hole in the wall to see if it would tell me how much money I had. I had been astounded at the figure that appeared when I finally found the button to press for *Balance*. Where had it all come from? I only had my pension. But I must have spent little over the years. I had no mortgage, ate little and spent nothing on pleasure. I felt like a rich woman. But it was still hard to get my head round today's prices. But I bought paint, which the girls slapped on the walls, as well as the floor, their hair, and anywhere else that got in the way.

When they had gone, promising to return next day to finish the work, I went into the kitchen to find a chair. The smell of paint followed me. I could not remember paint smelling quite so unpleasant. It used to be clean, not so chemical. Today it seemed not only to invade my nose, it crept into my mouth, down my throat. It promised to wipe out the past, offered a brighter future, but was still suffocating, threatening. I remembered reading that paint was bad for unborn babies. Kayleigh must stay out of the house while it was being painted, not move in until the fumes cleared.

I recognised the menace behind the cleanliness: I was exploiting the girls. They worked without pay. Smell told me that no one would believe they were doing it for Kayleigh.

'I know that,' said Smell, 'but not everyone will be so understanding.'

I shivered, and went to open the window letting in the sunlight, letting out the fumes, which nevertheless seemed to be taking over the house.

Smell mocked me, 'I'm not going out that way. Not experts are they, your Krew? They ought to pay you, the mess they're making.'

I tried to escape upstairs, but Smell followed.

I closed my ears, shut my eyes but powerful, impertinent Smell chased over my eyelids, and danced into my head, invading, mocking. I only needed to keep him out for a while. He would disappear when the girls returned, but meanwhile I was his slave.

'Prison,' he reminded me. 'You said you might as well be in prison, your life was meaningless. Now you've got these girls to dance attention on you, repaint and clean your house. How did you manage that? They'd never do a minute's cleaning in their own homes.'

'Go away. Go away. I know all that.'

'You can't go on like this you know. Sooner or later someone will discover where Kayleigh is, then what'll you do?'

'I'll deal with that when it happens.'

'Best to be prepared, like a good Boy Scout. Michael was a Scout, wasn't he?'

'What do you know about Michael?'

'You'd be surprised at the things I know about you and your family.'

'Get out of my head. You're making me ill.'

'I'm only telling you the truth,' said Smell. 'You're making yourself ill. You can't change these girls. Kayleigh will never be able to look after a baby, you know that. D'you hope she'll leave it with you, then you can have a child to look after again? What an idea. You won't live to see it grow up. You got yourself into this mess. But you can't get out so easily. You'll go to prison!'

I jumped up and tried to hit the smell in my head with the rolling pin, a muscle in my back protested, I winced.

'Will you just get out!'

'What if I don't?'

'I'll … I'll …'

'Ha, ha, there's nothing you can do is there? Ha, ha.'

That evening, in bed, Smell overpowered me again, then slowly gave way to Worry, who had left me in peace for some time; he was still as ugly. A great black cobweb binding me up, paralysing me, invading my mind, making thought impossible. Worry always rushed ahead, imagining the worst; monstrously magnifying anything that might be wrong; ignoring the obvious in favour of the improbable, the unlikely, the wildest reaches of imagination.

'You realise you've invited me in again, with Kayleigh?' said Worry. 'We go together, me and children. Kayleigh is a child. A child with child.' He chortled at his joke. I had to let him settle on my chest, as he used to, and he snuggled in as if he had never been away. 'That's better. You were always a soft place to rest me head.'

Now I resigned myself to more years of worry, about Kayleigh, her baby, even about myself perhaps: would I go to prison? I was guilty. What if someone had abducted John or Michael? But Kayleigh's mother could not be compared to me, could she? Worry snuggled closer, this was familiar, if not comfortable. He was at least weakening the power of Grief.

Earlier, prison had seemed preferable to an empty catless life. Now my life was full, full of girls, of Kayleigh's passionate anger, outbursts of weeping, unpredictability. My comfortable squalor was giving way to … I had no idea what was coming. Worry fell asleep before me, I luxuriated in the silence.

* * *

'There was a phone call for you dear, but we thought it best not to wake you. Kayleigh sends her love.'

Kayleigh! She hasn't been Kayleigh for a long time, years perhaps. When did she become Kay? And how? I didn't really notice, we were all so busy looking after Mark. She changed, and I hardly noticed. Those last few years, they dissolve into a rush of … of what? Of fulfilment? They make up for the wasted years of mourning. Yet, those years, too, are not wasted. Without them I might not have been able to help Kay and Mark as I did. How do you send love? I love Kay; she loves me. I'd never thought of this before, but we love each other. That's all there is. How does she know where I am?

* * *

I remember the day Kay found one of my poems. I knew then that she would go far. She read it aloud, struggling with my handwriting. I was never happy with my handwriting, it was part of myself, somewhat illegible. For years I never used it, then, when I needed it again, it seemed different, another me, perhaps more acceptable than the last. It no longer bothered me. Kayleigh read:

'Islands
Changeless, yet ever changing,
Buffeted by our relentless churning seas,
Tickled by the sands of time,
We stand.
Grounded in the healing peace of
The Great Green Deep,
Where all are one.'

'What's that all about, Mau?'
'It's an island speaking. Inspired by your Tip.'
'Our Tip wasn't an island. No sea. It was just a convenient place for us to hang out and have a moan.'

'I always saw it as an island of hope in the seas of hopelessness, of care in a heartless world. Somewhere set apart.'

'We had to cross the railway lines to get there.'

'Yes – a metaphorical sea. You can have an island in your heart as well as in the sea, Kay.'

'Railway lines in your heart? Weird. Is it a poem?'

'I hope so.'

'What's the Great Green Deep, Mau?'

'I'm not sure.'

'You wrote it.'

'It's what you found on your Tip. You all supported each other, helped each other. That's what I was trying to say.'

The Tip was surely more than somewhere to hang out and have a moan. Would they be able to create magic islands throughout their lives? Perhaps the real magic was within each one of them. Each one an island, and like islands, each, in some mysterious way, linked deep beneath the oceans. No one is an island. These links must surely survive.

'Poetry's weird, Mau. I'll stick to psychology, Mau.'

She had just started at college, doing A level psychology and sociology. She had thoughts of being a social worker: I could not think of anyone else who would make a better social worker.

'Some people think psychology's weird, Kay.'

'Yeah, but you can understand psychology, can't you?'

'I'm not sure I can. I'll stick with poetry. You don't have to understand that.'

I would have liked to live to see her graduate, of course I would. But by living on I would deny her that chance. She wouldn't put me in a home. If I insisted, would I have to sell my house to pay the fees? I've bequeathed my house to Kay and Mark. They could invite Sue to come and live with them. Get away from her parents. Help care for Mark. I put so much thought into organising it all. I didn't want her success at college and university to be overshadowed by my decline into total helplessness: unable at last to swallow or to breathe. Far better to go with dignity, to slip away into the peace of nature before Kay realised what was happening.

'Getting clumsy in your old age, Maude,' she said when I dropped a tea pot full of scalding water.

'Whoops a daisy, Maude, look where you're going, please,' when I fell for no reason.

But I couldn't hide it much longer. Would the hospital discover? Would they tell her? Would they contact my doctor? So many questions. No energy to think. I so nearly achieved my goal, now peace has been snatched from me ... I once wanted to go to college. Father laughed ...

I remember the old Kayleigh, she had changed so much over the years. The first week had been very hard for us both. It was not just the music, the dirty dishes, Kayleigh lying in bed till nearly mid-day. I was actually glad to have the house to myself all morning, but I was still irritated. Laziness was such a waste of life. It had infuriated Husband when the boys were Kayleigh's age.

I knew pregnant women needed to rest and teenagers proverbially got up late, and Kayleigh was both, but in some deep recess of my mind laziness was a sin. We had to give and take.

'Why is it that you are doing all the giving, Kayleigh the taking,' asked Resentment, building up in me. I suspected that Doubt had moved in with Kayleigh, when she moved in with me. She kept him well hidden, but sometimes he surfaced, often in the early hours. I thought he must say things like, 'What d'you think you're doing here?' Growling he might add, 'You mad or something?'

We did try to compromise, managed not to fight too often, but sometimes it felt like trying to stay upright walking on partially thawed mud. Kayleigh's constant cry was, 'Maude, I wish you wouldn't keep going on at me. Does me fucking head in.' She made dramatic exits from time to time, slamming the front door shouting, 'Just 'cos you lets me live in this crap dump don't mean you owns me.'

I had insisted on taking her to see her doctor; I said she could only stay with me if she did. It was for the sake of the baby. After sulks and tantrums, Kayleigh finally agreed, although terrified that the doctor might tell Them. I had got myself a new dress from Oxfam, a bit more up-market than my normal charity shops. I tied my hair back into a tight bun, which emphasised my wrinkles, but gave me a responsible look, I thought. I told Kayleigh not to wear make up. I was afraid she might run away as we sat in the awkward silence of the waiting room. Kayleigh idly flicked over the pages of a motherhood magazine, while I gazed at the posters overflowing from the notice boards. Kayleigh was not good at waiting. I couldn't remember the last time I'd felt impatient. Kayleigh's impatience was enough for two, for the whole waiting room. On two occasions I had to restrain her, when she jumped up saying, 'I'm off. If he don't want to see me, then I'm fucked if I want to see him.' I tried to ignore the looks of the other patients.

The doctor turned out to be an efficient young woman; how could one so young be a doctor? I thought doctors were men, and older than their patients. We said Kayleigh was my niece, come to stay. The doctor asked Kayleigh when her last period was. Kayleigh was as unhelpful as possible.

'Do it matter?' she asked.

'We need to know how far advanced your pregnancy is. I'm afraid it may be too late for a termination.'

'Termination?'

'Abortion.'

Kayleigh was shocked out of her half comatose state into one of horror. 'I didn't say nothing about no fucking abortion! Me Aunty Maude told me to come to you so's you could fix up about the hospital. And she said I'd get money for me and the baby off of the social.'

'Kayleigh!' I said, embarrassed that she swore in front of the doctor.

'You're very young to have a baby, Kayleigh.'

'So what? Romeo and Juliet was younger than me.'

'Romeo and Juliet were fiction, Kayleigh. And they didn't have a baby.'

'They would have, more than likely if they hadn't topped themselves.'

'What does your mother say?'

'I lives with me Aunty Maude. She's gonna help me.'

'You really want to keep the baby?'

'Why not? You had any babies?'

'Have you any idea how to look after a baby?'

'Maude knows. She's had two, but one's dead. The other buggered off, like her husband. That's why she wants to help me. Me mum good as turned me out, she's in Bristol,' she said, hoping to throw Them off the scent.

'Are you happy with this arrangement?' the doctor asked me. I was blushing at how well Kayleigh understood my motives.

'Not happy, doctor, but I'm willing to do my best to help Kayleigh.'

'I'll send you to the hospital for a scan,' said the doctor, 'then we'll know when the baby's due. Now, what about the baby's father?'

'What about him?'

'Does he know about his baby?'

'It's not his baby. It's mine.'

'You perfectly well know, Kayleigh, it takes two to make a baby. Is he going to help to support it?'

'Dunno know who he is.'

'You don't look the kind of girl who goes around with lots of different boys.' The doctor looked at Kayleigh, without make up she looked so young, so innocent.

'I doesn't. There was only this one. And he weren't a boy. He were a man. A horrid man. He grabbed me, raped me. Dunno who he is, don't want to. I were drunk. He were drunk. It's my baby.'

'That man committed a crime, Kayleigh. You're under age. He raped you. The police will want to know, find him, make sure he's punished, and helps to support his baby.'

'If he's a criminal I don't want him near me baby. Like I said, it's mine, not his. We'll cope. Aunty Maude and me, know what I means?'

The doctor, too busy to question this, working hard not to show her indignation at yet another teenage pregnancy coming too late for termination, accepted the story, gave her a booklet about how babies grow, get out, and how to look after them, told her to eat plenty of fruit and vegetables, ignoring the disgust on Kayleigh's face, get plenty of exercise and take some sort of acid pills. The last sounded a bit dodgy; Kayleigh decided to ignore it …

Was I now one of the Krew? How come they'd let an adult in? I knew I was not really an adult, did not belong in the adult world, any more than they belonged in the world of affluent teenagers. Slowly Kayleigh began to feel safe with me.

* * *

There is so much noise, clatter, chatter; no one hears me when I ask for a glass of water. There is no peace. There is no peace.

'This is a hospital, we are busy.'

It's as noisy as a prison. I thought I might have ended up in prison, would that have been so much worse than ending up here?

* * *

I remember that I hadn't realised, when I offered Kayleigh a home, that the whole Krew would feel themselves included in the invitation. I should have done. But they came all the time, listening to that raucous music, eating my biscuits. Once, exhausted and more than usually exasperated, I had said something about not having invited the whole Krew to live with me, and instantly regretted it. Kayleigh burst into an emotional tirade about her friends, my meanness, 'only a bit of fun'. It had ended in Kayleigh's dramatic exit, slamming the front door shouting, 'Just 'cos you lets me live here don't give you the right to tell me how to live me life. I don't tell you what to do!'

She did, I reflected, increasingly. I understood now what the words 'flounced out' meant. Boys don't flounce. I was always expecting, when tempers flared, as they did frequently, to be accused of exploiting the Krew, using them as cheap labour to renovate my house. To my surprise they never did.

Suze seemed to have a calming influence. She brought Kayleigh a pair of bootees she had knitted. Kayleigh looked at them, trying to find the right words, finally said, 'I thinks her feet'll be the same size, Suze.'

'I wouldn't be too sure, Kayles.'

Resentment reappeared from behind Worry. It was a long time since he'd troubled me, not since Husband left.

'You'd think they'd at least be grateful,' said Resentment. 'They move into your house, into your life, they turn everything up-side-down ...'

'It needed turning.'

'Yes – but like this? You can't call your life your own any more, can you?'

I tried to chase him away, but he stayed on in a corner, skulking, making me feel bad, unable to appreciate my new life. The girls seemed slightly more law abiding, now that they had to be so careful to keep Kayleigh's whereabouts secret.

'Don't fool yourself,' sneered Resentment, 'these girls are beyond hope. They chose to be the way they are.'

'They've got terrible backgrounds.'

'Not everyone from such families drops out or turns to crime.'

'Don't they? How do you know? These girls work so hard not to be sucked into it all.'

'Into what? What do you care? Do you care?'

'I don't know.'

Resentment was quiet for a while; I remembered his ugly prickles, so hard to remove, the way his seeds grew so quickly.

Once they took root they sprouted, blocked out joy and love, dried up reason, which was struggling to emerge from the recesses of my being.

The way that Kayleigh used to wander downstairs, settle herself heavily into the arm chair, pick up the remote control and flick through the TV programmes irritated me for some reason. I never switched on the TV without first consulting the Radio Times. I had learned to ignore Kayleigh's TV, and on the rare occasions I really wanted to see a programme, Kayleigh generally acquiesced without much fuss. Sometimes we watched together, with Kayleigh commenting all the way through the programme, 'Not more penguins! Haven't you had enough of them yet?' or 'Mau, do we have to have this on? Them animals gets up to some dirty things.'

'Nonsense, they're just like us,' I said: what a mixture of prudery and prurience Kayleigh was …

Guilt told me, yet again, that I should have persuaded Kayleigh to have an abortion.

I was still agonising over whether I was doing the right thing. It was too late now for second, third or fourth thoughts. I had made the offer so carelessly, thoughtlessly without considering how both our lives would be changed. Sometimes Kayleigh sobbed for her lost childhood. Then I suffered from Worry as never before in my life. 'What the fuck were you thinking of?' He was beginning to talk like Kayleigh. He constantly questioned my motives, cackling infuriatingly. I told him to,

'Shut up,' once to 'Fuck off.' The girls were bad enough, driving me to distraction with their music, their mess, their giggling. I didn't need Worry. Yet I knew my house was alive again, and tried to hide this from Worry.

Both Kayleigh and I were aware, if dimly, that we were living with the consequences of decisions taken too carelessly. Kayleigh came back from the Tip one day and threw her arms round me, saying, 'Thanks, Mau.'

'What for?'

'We could never have had the baby in the Shack.'

'No, you'd have realised that soon enough.'

'Dunno. It's cool here, Mau. I feels safe here.'

'Good.'

* * *

It's so hot and stuffy here. I need to be back on the Moor. The clean, clear air, to be part of it all. I need to be out of this smell. Schools, hospitals, prisons, they have something in common – what is it? Each has its own distinctive, and very different smell, none of them pleasant.

* * *

I remember the safety of my childhood, when this was Gran's house. I can still smell it: oil lamps mixed with lavender, from the lavender bags Gran made for church sales of work. Gran, born so long ago, even before the twentieth century began, had no electricity or gas and only a cold tap in the house. Paraffin lamps cast a warm, living light, open fires spat in friendship. In winter, life at Gran's was hard: when it was really cold she put the tall black paraffin stove in my bedroom, and I went to sleep watching the flower patterns on the greying ceiling, breathing in the comforting warm smell.

Over the years, since the house had been mine, its smell had changed with my changing life. In the early years of marriage there was the sickly warm smell of breast milk, vomit and the scrambled-egg yellow of dirty nappies. Intermittently it smelled of paint and turps, with Husband's forays into doing it himself. Slowly, the smells changed to muddy football boots mingled with an indecipherable scent of dirty socks, bloody knees and cheap sweets. When the boys were teenagers, the smell changed again to chips, joined eventually by the deadly odour of motorbike oil. Finally, when I was alone, the musty, overpowering scent of tom cats, mingled with decay: a friendly autumn rot wafted in from the garden to join the more sinister moulds of unwashed clothes, unmade bed and dirty hair. Only dimly aware of all the changes, I no longer cared what it smelled of.

The disintegration of house and garden was gradual. It ceased to be a home quite quickly, probably when John left, after which it housed Husband and me. When he went, it became a mere shelter, a container for me, the cats and Grief. The grey pall that spread itself over my whole life, now invaded house and garden.

I could never quite understand, and certainly not explain, the special bond between me and Gran in those long war years when Mother had been rushed off to the TB sanatorium. I soon found compensations for living in the city: Gran and Granddad. Granddad was kind, but Gran was … Gran. Special, dependable. I can't explain what that means, or that very special kind of love. Gran never needed to scold. I didn't wet the bed at Gran's, and always blessed her for the joy of waking up in a dry bed, the watery dreams of rivers which came true in such a horrible way vanished. I knew why Gran wanted me to have her house.

As I aged, I saw my contemporaries become Grans, and yearned to share again that very particular kind of belonging. I ached for grandchildren: it was part of my mourning for Michael, part of my hope to see John again, of my hatred of Husband, who might be a Granddad. I watched Grans at half terms and after school, looking after grandchildren. What sort of Gran would I have been? I tried to visualise John's children: would I recognise them if I met them in the street? Ridiculous idea. I would not even recognise John. He was a grey stranger now.

Sometimes I felt that Mark was my grandson, that the special relationship I had with Gran could perhaps have been recreated with him. But this was ridiculous: Kay was more of my granddaughter than a daughter in age, and certainly my relationship with her was nothing like mine with Gran. But I felt her as the daughter I never had. I shared in the bringing up of Mark. I helped her with the breast feeding. I was there for her when he was born.

Gran had a lot of pain at the end of her life, like me …

I remembered her that day, when I'd offered Kayleigh my home, Gran's home. I got up stiffly, painfully, and walked slowly home, to a home that seemed to be going to be Kayleigh's. Was I going out of my mind? What had I done? Why? I had invited Kayleigh into my home. How on earth had I got myself into this mess, and more importantly, how could I get out of it? I was frightened. I had been beginning to feel my mind picking up its dropped stitches, to knit up the unravelling threads of my existence, but I wasn't ready for this. I'd been forced into making a decision, something I'd not done for years. It hurt. No. The decision had made itself, it came from nowhere. I'd got into the habit of just letting life happen to me, now I needed to take action: make a choice.

This was the first choice I'd made since … since when? Michael's death? John's leaving? Husband's divorce? When had I last freely chosen to do anything? Now I'd made a really stupid choice. I was terrified of the idea of someone else in my life, in my home, and did it have to be Kayleigh? It would not be my home any more, not my life any more. But my home and my life were no longer of much use to me. There was no going back. I was embarking on a terrifying journey into uncertainty.

After sitting so long on a milk crate, my arthritis had started protesting. Pain once more. I accepted him, felt I deserved him:

what right had I to be alive, let alone healthy, when my son was dead? Pain and I knew each other well.

The girls watched me go.

I walked home even more slowly than usual.

We're poles apart, Kayleigh and me, I thought, and a distant physics lesson shot up from my memory. 'Unlike poles attract,' I had copied tidily, delighting in the dance of the iron filings on the paper, under the magnet's hidden control. Take the magnet away and the magic grey patterns collapsed.

It was long after I reached home that I collected myself enough to put the kettle on. Not even a cat to comfort me. Tiddly would have helped me decide. But if he was still alive I would not be making this decision. I begged my tired mind to help me, to exert itself, as I had not asked it to do for years. The kettle boiled, steam rising, like the promise of a summer early morning mist. I did not notice.

I started to cry, forgetting the tea, went into the sitting room, sank into my chair, and saw Michael's face smiling out from all those photographs, which for years I passed unseeing. Where had all the smiles gone?

Should I rejoice that I had asked Kayleigh to come and put an end to my loneliness? I saw Kayleigh smiling at home, a child on her hip, making tea one-handed, as I had once done. When had I seen Kayleigh smile? I saw my kitchen sink piled with dirty dishes, uneaten meals congealing on them. I would have to tell Kayleigh that I'd made a bad mistake.

What am I to do, I wondered. I ought to be sensible. What's that? Go to Kayleigh's parents and tell them she's pregnant? I didn't even know where they lived, and she'd never have forgiven me. Why would that matter? Could I leave Kayleigh and her Krew, let them cope with it all? Think she can have a baby in the Shack? They must know that's not an option. Should I go to social services? I wouldn't know how to start.

What was the alternative? I had to offer her a home. I'd be guilty of something. Child abduction? Kayleigh's a child, technically. Kidnap? Not if she had wanted to come. Aiding and abetting? Would that matter? What mattered was that the child would have some sort of a start in life: Kayleigh would have someone with experience of children to help her. I had been a good mother when the boys were little. All babies need is love, Kayleigh already seemed to love the baby. It was the only thing to do, the right thing to do.

I would be guilty of some crime, might go to prison; not pleasant, but my life was not pleasant. One could have a cat in prison. Or was it a canary? Either would do. I had been locked up with Grief for so long I might as well be locked up in prison.

The warm smell of hot metal came from the kitchen, I had been dimly aware that the room was filling with steam, but could only think of one thing at a time. I remembered the kettle, and rushed to rescue it, grabbed it from the gas, it was red hot, burnt my hand. I dropped it, narrowly missing my foot. Where would I have to go for a new kettle?

Who else would offer Kayleigh a home if I didn't? This had been my home as a child, and as a mother; denied grandmothering, I could at least share with Kayleigh the joys of motherhood. As I turned the problem over and over in my mind, I began to glimpse my former self, remembering what it meant to be a mother: broken nights for years, not weeks; then the banging of the front door as they came home from school. 'Mum, I'm starving'; school uniforms to be hastily cleaned before next morning; conkers forgotten in the oven, the kitchen filled with acrid fumes; birthday cakes with candles that seemed impossible to blow out; disagreements, arguments, fights even; bruised knees; high temperatures at two am; vomit; girlfriends. I had enjoyed motherhood, despite my own mother's views on childrearing. 'You'll spoil them,' I heard Mother say.

I had found it hard not to spoil. It involved so much crying; my heart would long to pick up and feed a hungry baby, but my mind told me to wait until ten o'clock. So I tried to raise my boys to know that their wishes counted for little in life, and to bury their feelings. I will not interfere with Kayleigh's mothering.

I had not allowed myself to think about motherhood for over twenty years; now it all came back to accuse me. Those years had been good years. Even the Tragedy could not wipe them out. This had been my life. Kayleigh was offering me the chance to live again. Why did I hesitate? It would bring back painful memories, but there would be joy as well. For years I had avoided both joy and pain. I might as well have killed myself. I always lacked the courage, or was it so that I might be available for Kayleigh that I never got past thinking about it? I sat in my filthy, neglected house, contemplating, hesitating, questioning.

Motherhood. The celebration of life. Kayleigh was so young, just a child, but she seemed attuned to motherliness, ready and eager for it. She would soon learn the universal language of mothers, as she learned the baby's different cries: quiet cries of weariness that would fade into sleep, angry cries of hurt, of hunger, of pain. I would teach Kayleigh the marvellous, dreadful meaning of motherhood as I myself found a new meaning in life. This was at last a practical way to help the girls.

If I didn't offer Kayleigh a home I wouldn't be able to go to the Tip any more. Would it be harder to have Kayleigh living here, or live without the Tip? The cats would miss me. But I could bring one home. I could hear the girls:

'What happened to Mau?'

'Dunno. She just went.'

'Didn't do what she promised, did she?'

'Did you think she would?'

'Nah.'

I would quickly be forgotten, just another of Them, the shadowy mass of adults who make promises they don't mean to keep. Who do not care. I never doubted that Kayleigh would accept my offer, she had already done so. Like a fly in a spider's web, I had been sucked into the Krew's web of caring. Creaking, unused parts of me were starting to move, unfamiliar emotions cautiously rising from the dying embers of my life. I had no choice. I went upstairs …

They were good girls, the Krew. Good girls. What happened to the others, I wonder. Where were they now?

* * *

Are my eyes shut or open? My eyelids are heavy, they must be shut, but I can see it all so clearly. So clearly. But what do I see? Where am I?

'Maude? … Maude? Can you hear me?'

I can, but don't seem able to answer. I try to nod my head, not sure if I've succeeded. Am I being uncooperative? That's what the Krew were called at school, as well as rude, and ungovernable. What does that say about the school?

'What medication are you taking, dear?'

Why should I be taking medication? There is nothing that will help me. Only death, and you're trying to prevent that. I try to shake my head … When words escape me, where do they go? Into the great white nothingness my tormentors came from? Is this where I should be now? Where I shall go, when I go? Peace.

* * *

I remember saying, so thoughtlessly, so carelessly, 'You can have the boys' room.' Easy to say. I had not opened that door for years then. What was inside? I pictured it: chaos, Michael's motorbike posters on the walls, oily bits of motorbike on yellowing newspaper all over the floor. John had always grumped that Michael took up far more than his fair share of the room. John's girlie pin ups had equal wall space, yet were overshadowed by motorbike paraphernalia. Michael and motorbikes: together in life, as in death. I stood outside the door, trembling. Could I go in? I was paralysed. I would leave it until tomorrow. Kayleigh was not coming until after lunch. No. I had to clear it tonight. I held the door handle firmly, determined to get it over with. Then stopped, stepped back, nearly falling down the stairs. I would have to get rid of all Michael's things. What could I do with them? Give them to charity shops, as I had with what Husband had left behind? I clung to the door handle again, clutching it like a lucky charm. A long pause. Could I? Once I was inside it would be easier, I told myself.

My hand finally opened the door and I stepped in carefully, with my eyes shut. I opened them looking at the floor, and saw the familiar linoleum, which the boys had badgered Husband to replace. I turned on the light; the bulb had gone. Then, bravely, I looked up. I gasped. Whatever had happened? The floor was clear: no motorbike bits; only lighter patches on bare walls showed where posters had once been. I stood confused.

Where was Michael? His motorbike bits? His mess? His posters? Was I going out of my mind?

I stood in the middle of the tidy room, unable to grasp it. Then memory hit me, with an almost physical blow: I collapsed on to the narrow bed, shocked out of my mind, drained of all feeling. All the years I had remembered something that did not exist. This was not Michael's room. It never had been. It had been the boys' room, then John's. I cursed my faithless memory.

Something else emerged from the hazy depths of forgetting. Suddenly, frighteningly clearly, I saw the quarrel on the evening of the Tragedy: Husband shouting, John watching, delighted, Michael defiant, buckling on his crash helmet and going out of the back door. Had Michael been going too fast because he was angry? What had the quarrel been about? I remembered him slamming the back door. Had his last words to me had been, 'Oh grow up, Mum.' Before that he had said something like, 'It's difficult with you as a mother.' What was? Were 'Take care,' or 'Do be careful' my last words to him, or were they, too, angry? What had I said to provoke that?

Now, I remembered following him, pleading with him, as he unlocked the garden shed and wheeled the monster into the tiny lane at the back.

I saw his frustration, his futile attempts to hurry the difficult manoeuvre. I was running after him. 'Please, Michael, please.' He ignored me; the roar as his anger fired the bike into life was more menacing than usual. I saw myself standing on the pavement watching the tail light disappearing, weeping with despair, then returning to the dark alleyway.

Did Husband say, 'That bike'll be the death of him,' as I came back to the comfort of the gas fire, or did I? I noticed a smirk on John's face, as I warmed myself. I saw it all now clearly, although it had been buried so deep, so long. The cause of the anger still escaped me, I did not want to know, and shrank from the scene. How far was I, or Husband, responsible for the defiance of that last great roar that marked the end of motherhood?

Then, seeing the reality of the room behind the closed door, I questioned the memory I had kept of that fateful evening. The faces of the police were etched into my mind, but so was the motorcycle presence in this room. Was anything real any more? If we are our memories, who was I? Yet the images were real, part of me, had shaped me over the years, made me who I was. Was I a mere creation of my own fantasy? Did I exist at all? I shivered. Doubt attacked me. Memory was a treacherous prankster.

I had been aware for some time that my memory was weakening, and could fail me. Perhaps I deserved this, for having wasted my mind. How did I let that happen? I had good O levels, but let myself become a stay-at-home mother.

Some years after Mark's birth, a tiny glimmer, a faint spark, appeared in my mind. As I gradually turned my face towards the human race, I realised that, whatever my infirmities, my mind still worked. I might need bifocal glasses, a stick to help me walk, but this didn't mean that my mind was decaying. I didn't feel confused. I was as capable of thought as I'd ever been.

Being over seventy didn't make me forgetful. Even before the Tragedy I'd forgotten things, after it I was not aware of forgetting. Perhaps the forgotten was best forgotten. It was not ridiculous to think of using my mind again. I knew I was too old ever to be a teacher. But I could study.

As I, very gradually, allowed this ambition to enter my mind, I felt a shiver pass through my body. My brain stirred back to life, like a pile of rotting leaves rustling in early spring wind. I could see them, leaves lower in the pile damp, scented with decay, no longer leaves, they rotted, they returned to the earth that made them. Leaves at the top stirred, fluttered and, if a particularly lively blast caught them, took off, flying, feeling once more the power of life, dancing to the music of spring. They came down eventually in a new position, with new views, new companions, before inevitably decaying in their turn. The upper reaches of my brain were fluttering, remembering. Why? said the voice of Reason, now reviving within me. 'Why not?' said the spark.

For some reason I didn't fully understand, I didn't tell Kayleigh about the poster I'd seen in the library advertising the Open University. I felt she'd given me permission when she decided to go to college. I was already a member of the University of the

Third Age, and had joined their poetry group. I picked up a leaflet, and filled in the form, and was glad that Kayleigh was out when the postman came with the large envelope. I hid it under my bed, opened it a few days later, when Kayleigh was out again. I initially considered English literature, but was fascinated by a course called *An Introduction to the Humanities*, including literature, history, philosophy, music and all kinds of other studies. All those new subjects were exciting, but it was a private excitement, not yet for sharing. I also hid the small notebook I'd bought from the Oxfam shop. Oxfam sold more than old clothes now. I saw shelves of second hand books, and other shelves of new items, among which my eye was caught by a book entitled *I used to be a cardboard box*. It sounded an interesting title, and I was at first disappointed to find it was an empty notebook. I bought it. It was up to me to write the book. At the bottom I read the words, 'Recycled into something Remarkable.'

I felt the wind blowing through me, cleansing, rocking, destroying, creating. Why not? Why not? I knew I was not too old to think. I couldn't tell Kayleigh yet. I guarded my Ambition, felt it tightening, growing stronger. Reason told me that the idea of studying at my age was ridiculous. Ambition and Reason battled it out: Ambition won. Reason accepted that Ambition was also reasonable. But for the moment the thick envelope remained under the bed. Could all be well?

That was not so long ago. How long? Time seemed uncertain these days. How long after Michael's death had John finally departed? How long had Husband and I been alone together in the house? We had once had such plans for what we would do when the children left: a second honeymoon on the Moor, even walking in the mountains of Scotland, something I had long dreamed of; finding new delights, a fruitful retirement and old age for us both. Where had these dreams gone? Burnt to ashes in the crematorium. How long had I spent alone? Years and years. It did not matter how many. How had I let this happen?

Of course John had lived here for months, or years, after Michael's death: had made it his room. Why had Memory cut that out? I stood silently in the emptied room. Emptied of memories, of Michael; John's tidiness had expunged his brother. He had had to make it his room, how could he have lived with Michael's passion? Why had I not realised this? The thought of getting rid of Michael's possessions had terrified me, now I realised I had also been looking forward to it. John must have done it for me, as I had no recollection of doing it. The reality of the empty room took him even further away.

How small this room was; the whole house was small. As a child it had not been small. I saw the room as a nursery: a cot, then a cot and a small bed. Husband and I had painted it a pale shade of yellow, and stencilled animal shapes on to the walls. The hole in the ceiling, made when I tried to fix up a mobile with farmyard animals, was still visible. Then there were two narrow beds, not much room for children let alone growing men. Now only one bed, no man.

I gazed at the denuded walls, and began to cry. Gently at first, then noisily, the tears flowed again as they had all those years ago. Hot, bitter tears of despair, recrimination, helplessness. Why had I chosen not to recognise what was going on in my life? What had it been like before the visit of the police? Memory stumbled. I could remember the days when I had been a parent of young children, and of teenagers. The time when my sons were young men had almost vanished. Why? Had disputes between Husband and me started before the Tragedy? How long before? Memory refused to answer. I worried, in a vague way, perhaps felt more that I should worry, than actually worried, whether I was getting Alzheimer's disease, that dark, shapeless threat lurking at the back of the mind of everyone over the age of around sixty. A threat that life could spin out of control. Mine had years ago.

I remembered … so much, and yet not enough. Mark's birth, Michael's death … Memory, I thought, that diaphanous, grey shawl, which covers us throughout our lives, lets most of our actions, emotions, thoughts float through her, holding on to what she considers important. Her warp and weft briefly shift, to hasten the passage of things she wants to let go or retain, her shape never quite as it was. Sometimes she is an angel, storing precious delights: a child's first word, or the glory of a green woodpecker who briefly graced the garden. Some things leave her permanently misshapen, spitting out the pleasure, preserving grudges, thoughtless words, fatal tragedies.

She colours herself with the patterns of our lives. In childhood we learn to control her, beseeching her to hold on to those things we need to remember: two and two make four. As we grow we burden her with scientific equations, philosophical theories. We try to bend her fabric, and she laughs at us, hiding desperately sought details. She works while we sleep, sifting and sorting, deciding what to release, what to bury. We shape her over the years, our now faithful, now capricious, companion. By old age she should have become so thick and dense that everything is retained, nothing can pass through this veil, so deeply encrusted with life. Perhaps, when the burden is too heavy, holes appear, important items fly away, and we are powerless to catch them? Why does she desert us when we most need her consolation? Have we treated her badly, expected too much of her? When we question her, she replies with her Mona Lisa smile, 'I have been shaped by you, now I shape you. You and I are one.'

I shuddered. What else have I misremembered?

* * *

I do not want to remember this hospital stay, my first time in over 70 years. I do not want to die here, where all is geared to the saving of life. I need to do it out on the Moor, where all lives and dies, and understands that death is part of life. I need to go now, while I still can. Babs believes that only God can decide when someone should die. She says I'll see Michael again one day in heaven: an obscene story invented to make grief bearable. Grief is not, should not be, bearable. I picture Michael with white wings, covered in motorbike oil, playing a harp. Could you play heavy metal on a harp? Do they have motorbikes in heaven? If not he would prefer hell: what's the point of being saved and going to heaven, if Michael is in hell? Life goes on: dead life.

* * *

I remember one day, soon after Kayleigh had moved in, before Mark was born, walking home from the co-op, I noticed a ramp leading to the door of the library. A woman was going up, pushing what I would have called a push chair, now called a 'Buggy', which sounds slightly insanitary. I followed with my trolley, the door opened automatically, and I went in. I knew it would be different, but was amazed and alarmed at the transformation. Videos. Computers. Where were the books?

I wandered past youths mesmerised by flickering computer screens into the reference section. Here I saw one old man who could have come from the days when I had the power to say, 'Take your wet jacket off, please sir, it's dripping all over the floor,' or, 'Silence, please.' I realised that but for my house, Gran's house, I could have been one of those who daily took refuge in the library. I was glad it was still performing this service.

I had stopped reading when Michael died, returned my library books and never came back. Sometimes, at home, I'd opened books I once found uplifting, but left them on the floor in piles that had stopped growing many years ago. Now, as I looked for the fiction section, I saw *Talking Books* and *Large Print*, even paperbacks, which I was sure were never purchased when I was a librarian. Where were the real books? I was in a foreign country again: talking books indeed. I took one down and realised that the case contained tapes. Were these for the blind or the illiterate? I put it back hastily, I did not want to be thought illiterate.

I found the fiction shelves eventually, and browsed through books by authors I had never heard of, hardly surprising as I had not read a book for over twenty years. Then I found a friend: Hardy. The living books, those that became part of one, were still there, jostling with all the rest. *Far from the Madding Crowd*: I'd loved that as a teenager, seen the film. Was that the one where sheep plunged to their deaths over the cliffs? The picture of that tragedy sprang vividly before my eyes, and I saw the face of faithful Gabriel Oak: 'When I look up there will you be ...' The words had brought tears to my eyes when Husband left, but now I thought, 'How boring.' I no longer wanted to look up and see Husband. I was reminded of a verse my mother often quoted: 'Two minds with but a single thought, two hearts that beat as one.' What a waste of two minds to be able only to produce a single thought. And that was, in all probability, his.

From now on I could think my own thoughts, and there would be more than one. Why not read Hardy again? Cleaning, washing, shopping did not fill my days, although so far Kayleigh never did any housework.

The girl behind the counter had probably not been born when I worked here, so I was not worried about being recognised. I filled in a membership card, but had to return later with a gas bill to confirm my address. Finally I took the book home. I managed to find my reading glasses, but realised that my eyes had changed in twenty years, so made an appointment and got myself a new pair of bifocals. How had I lived for so long without reading?

I took to spending more and more time in my bedroom, I never got round to painting it, but had cleaned it, found new curtains and a rug in the market; installed a bookcase. Sitting in the rocking chair with a cup of tea, I escaped into long forgotten stories, gradually moving on to look at some of the modern books, most of which I gave up after a few pages, but some took me to places I wanted to explore. The modern world slowly began to make sense. Altercations with Kayleigh fell in importance. Worry, asking me what I would do if Kayleigh's parents eventually appeared, ceased to wake me at night.

I was also spending more time in the library, growing used to what the word 'library' now meant. I didn't dare to try the computers, but I surreptitiously watched others, thought I might have a go one day. I read the notices, and saw one about the U3A. The idea excited me, and I enrolled on a literature group, and found myself volunteering to interview a local poet and present a biography to the next meeting. To my amazement I was not nervous. Kayleigh could not see the point of 'going to school' when one was old, but she humoured me: I was, of course, a bit off my rocker. This was harmless: let her go to school if it keeps her happy. I tried to tell Kayleigh how inspired I had been by the poet's insistence that anyone could write poetry. 'I just catch the poems, I don't know where they come from,' she had said. 'All I do is write them down, then hone them into shape. The perspiration that comes after the inspiration is all I do, Maude.'

I started trying to catch poems; at first they were all about Michael, and I didn't want to catch them. Then one day I saw the dirt dancing in a shaft of spring sunlight and fetched my new notebook. It was a very short poem, but full of joy, of life. Michael, I realised with surprise, would not want me to waste what life I had left. Michael had been retreating into the shadows ever since Kayleigh moved in, perhaps that was where he belonged. Since the Tragedy he had never been far away, angry, full of recrimination, feeding my bitterness. I could sense him now approving of Kayleigh: would he have fancied her? I knew that nothing would ever heal my hurt, and I still didn't want it healed, but it was changing. Anger was giving way to acceptance. All could be well. I found my pen, and caught a poem of peace. I wanted to share it. Kayleigh might say, 'Cool', rather than 'So?' if she liked it. Suze would probably say it was 'nice'. It was not nice. Peace was disturbing.

Could I share it with my U3A literature group? No, they looked at Great Literature. I got out the programme: there was a 'poetry workshop'. Poetry as work was a new idea. Did I want to work at poetry?

Could the boys' room become once more a nursery? At least it was clean, tidy, ready for Kayleigh. I shut the door, and went to my own room; the contrast hit me. After the musty scent of orderliness there I recognised in my room the odour of my unwashed body, saw the greyness of the sheets: when had I last washed them? An old rocking chair where I had once sat at night feeding hungry babies, soothing teething sons, comforting the bad dreams of childhood, was overflowing with dirty clothes, which spilled on to the floor. The wardrobe door was open, as was every drawer in the chest. Instead of washing clothes I would buy new ones at charity shops, so the smell in the room was that of many strangers, as well as mine. How had I slept with this stench every night for so long? How on earth was I going to clean this up? Why bother? I could still tell Kayleigh it had all been a big mistake.

I gazed at an old woollen jumper I had once been fond of, its threads unravelling, tangled. It came from the era of jumble sales, those precursors of the charity shop. I remembered watching the queues forming long before the doors of the church hall were opened, and the benevolent allowed the poor in, to scrabble amongst the cast off of the less poor. I remembered pulling it out from a pile of other smelly jumpers on the table, captivated by the colours: dark reds, browns, greens. Life seemed to shine out of it then. It was obviously hand-knitted, with love, lovingly fitted for some smiling face, admired by friends, 'Will you knit me one?' Now, abused and abandoned, it lay discarded and decaying, its pure wool matted and thickened. Its colours took me back to the days when I had helped Granddad, as he conjured every shade of green from tiny brown seeds, lovingly placed in a darker brown soil, and covered with darkness. As a child I had always been able to see those tiny brown seeds at the heart of the green vegetables, as I helped them grow, gently uprooting weeds, poisoning slugs. Runner beans rewarded us by rushing up the poles Granddad planted for them, and covering themselves with bright red flowers, redder than anything in the jumper. Tender lettuces stayed close to the forgiving brown soil, smelling of the life which nurtured them. I looked at the jumper, finally discarded when the hole in the elbow met one at the wrist, it seemed to be unravelling as I watched. Kayleigh could not come in here. Here I could keep my comfortable chaos, have this one room of squalor to retreat to. I pictured myself closing the door on the rest of the tidy house, once more like the one I recalled from the ordered safety of my childhood, returning to my private disorder, the comfort of my old age, and my misery. I kicked at the ancient jumper, dust rose in the filtered sunlight, and subsided. I would need to lock the door. My eyes moved to the greasy grey sheets and the pile of discoloured blankets under which my misery hid itself at night, and thought of the tidily folded blankets on John's – Kayleigh's – bed.

A light breeze blew the door ajar, it never opened properly, because of the piles of clothing on the floor. For a moment I thought a cat was coming in, but it was only the wind, I could see the telephone wires moving silently: another life outside. I sat listening to it. The words of a poem rose from my childhood, as poetry so often did. 'Not I, but the wind blows through me ...' Was it D.H. Laurence? It was safer, more comfortable to keep the wind out. I rocked gently in my chair, feeling my mind trying to surface, to come up through the years of neglect. It had been a good mind once, I remembered. I'd used it to shape family life. That was past. I was old, too old. Too old for what? Thoughts were occurring to me, I was finding it harder to ignore them, subdue them, send them back. My mind was demanding attention.

I slept, but woke in the middle of the night and lay there trying to imagine the boys' room occupied by Kayleigh and her baby. Now the idea of Kayleigh moving in seemed impossible. All I really needed was another cat. Why had I not immediately gone to the pet shop when Tiddly disappeared? It would have been a betrayal. I could not replace Tiddly, any more than I could replace Michael.

Kayleigh would not be a replacement, she would only be temporary. She would naturally move on, but would stay in touch, would visit. I would baby sit, help the child with her homework, love them both and be loved. I half drifted back to sleep, and half dreamed, half remembered again, the quiet pleasures of motherhood. My mind moved on to how Grief and suffering had sustained me over the years.

I fell asleep again, and woke early. The gap between going to bed and getting up was an increasingly brief respite from unhappiness. I still half hoped to find Tiddly when I woke, purring as usual, apologising, receiving automatic absolution. In sleep these past weeks, I had been aware of searching, turning over my stony solitude, unsure what I needed to find.

Surfacing from the dream – was it a dream? – I had already forgotten it: something was different this morning. My brain struggled. No cat. It was still hard to be alone in the morning with no warm, soft weight that purred itself, and me, back to life. I would probably look for a cat on the bed for as long as I lived. That was not what was different: Kayleigh. My decision. The morning light showed me again the chaos of my life. I decided to go back to sleep.

But sleep is not something to make decisions about, it has a will of its own; like a cat, it may decide to come to your bed, if it does not there is nothing to be done. As I slowly accepted wakefulness, I returned to the decision: could I possibly have Kayleigh living here? Did I want to clear up, to tidy, to clean each day as I once did? The choice was mine. I drifted off again, briefly, and woke with a headache. Had I been dreaming or thinking?

Both things I had not done for years. Kayleigh's coming would mean that I had to learn to think, and to dream, again.

When I got up I looked around my sitting room, at the dirt, the neglect. How long had it been like this? Was this why Husband had gone?

I set off for the shops. Could I do it? Regular meals, washing, cleaning, talking: all the things that had once woven themselves into a life. Could I ever return to that mundane pleasurable existence? A child again in the boys' room. New life playing in the garden, learning to climb the stairs. Laughing and crying. Cutting teeth. Learning to talk. Welcoming life. A tiny baby, so much more vulnerable than my large strong son, to be sheltered, protected. I narrowly missed the dog mess; I would have to learn to look where I was going.

* * *

All so long ago now. It would be so wonderful to sink back to … to where? To where I was when I nearly died. That bloody dog … All my careful planning ruined. How right I was to choose death on the Moor. Watched over by vast granite tors. Birds singing their morning chorus. All that makes life worth living was there for my death. I have been cheated: taken back to a life that will become increasingly not worth living.

'Nurse? Could you get me some water?' She doesn't appear to hear me.

'We'll soon have you home, Maude.'

I don't think so. No resurrection for me. We all have to die sometime, sooner or later. Don't those who work in hospitals realise this? It was far too soon for Michael, I fear it will be too late for me … In a way Kayleigh was resurrected, reborn after Mark's birth, and so was I, but now I need to go …

* * *

I remember that day she finally agreed to go home. I'd come to the hospital, bringing grapes, not knowing what to expect. She'd been asked a few times about going home, but had always turned away and buried her head in the pillows. I was wondering how many more days I would trail over to the hospital to see her sulk and flounce about. For the first time she was out of bed, and looked as if she had had a shower.

'I want to go home, Mau.'

I stopped breathing.

'Yes … and Baby?'

'Mark can come too. Just till I makes me mind up.'

I held back a huge sigh of relief. My home would hold a baby again, if only briefly.

'It's a lovely name.' Any name would have been lovely.

This was so different from the day before, when nothing I could say seemed to lift her misery at what she had become.

Then she had wailed, 'I don't want to be a mother.'

'You knew you'd be a mother if you had a baby. You're not stupid.'

'Yeah. But I didn't know it'd be like this.'

'Like what?'

Kayleigh got cross. 'I told you. I dunno. Weird.'

'You'll get used to it.'

'I don't want to get used to it. I want to be like I was before. Not a mum.'

'You said you'd be a different sort of mum.'

Kayleigh was silent for a while. 'I won't be like my fucking mum, that's for sure.'

'No. You couldn't if you tried. You'll always be you. Kayleigh. But a Kayleigh who's a mother.'

Kayleigh's tears rose to a crescendo. 'If I comes home with you, and leaves him here … that wouldn't make me like I used to be?'

'Kayleigh, you've been changing for nine months. Even if you'd had an abortion you'd still have changed. We can never go back.'

I remembered the long discussions about abortion in the Shack, all those months ago: Kayleigh's determination to have the baby, insisting it was crying out to be born, to be loved. Now he was trying to claim that love, which seemed to have evaporated. Kayleigh's terrified face, wet with tears, looked as childlike as Mark's. She hiccuped as the boys used to when stopping crying as children …

She looked quite different today, somehow. Birth and death both change things; life is never the same after either. I remembered the horror of first hearing of the Tragedy: the diffident young policemen, one a woman, who had come with the news, embarrassed by my screams. Husband embarrassed. Someone said, 'There, there,' which only made me scream louder. What did that mean? I did a lot of screaming.

'It won't bring him back,' Husband said. As if I didn't know.

The shock took my breath away. Left me gasping. I fell over. Husband was holding me. So close. We had not been so close since the early days of our marriage, but this was a different closeness. He laid me on the sofa and rushed to find a glass of water. I felt a surge of relief as momentarily he left the room. I didn't want him there, I wanted to be able to scream.

Screaming helped because it left me too exhausted to think; gave me space. As I screamed I felt the whole world screaming with me, all life united in screaming against the ending of one young life, for all life is one. I heard Husband and the policemen saying things, part of me told me to listen to them. Why wasn't Husband screaming with me, instead of trying to stop me? He should be screaming, this was his child too. Eventually the screaming had given way to silent grief, then the need to tell the whole world. I had few friends to tell. I tried to talk to a neighbour, but she was embarrassed, changed the subject. One cannot talk about the death of a child: Michael was still a child, though no longer a child.

Would the Krew let me tell them about Michael? They were only children. They might decide they didn't want me in their space if I talked about death; a dead cat was all right, but a dead child.

I remembered that they had their own dead child to talk about. Charley had been killed on a road. The Krew blamed the teacher who had sent her out of the room a few minutes before the accident. The girls talked a lot about funerals. I was astonished at how many funerals they had been to, more than I had. I couldn't remember going to any as a teenager: my friends and relations didn't kill themselves, take overdoses, take away and crash cars; babies didn't die of meningitis or cot deaths when I was young …

Mark was screaming now, a nurse would be in any moment to see what was wrong, Kayleigh turned to the cot.

'You gets on me tits, you does. They're dribbling again, Mau, just when I'd got myself cleaned up.'

Mark cried even louder. I waited. Should I pick him up? I felt as if I were walking on a knife-edge. One wrong move, wrong word from me, and all could be lost. Mark's crying grew louder, more desperate. Who could ignore it? Eventually even Kayleigh sighed, put down her comb, picked up the angry child, and settled herself on the chair. 'We're going to have to put a stop to this,' she said. I tried not to wonder what 'this' was. But she just put Mark to her breast.

'Me tits ain't me own any more. They does what they fucking wants.'

'They do it for Mark,' I said

'Yeah.' She looked at her son, for the first time without even a lingering trace of revulsion. Mark and Kayleigh: bound to each other by milk and blood. Had she done this to her mum? She knew she'd been bottle fed, her mum couldn't be doing with all this mess, she'd said bottles were cleaner, more hygienic. Mark sucked placidly and a wave of what might have been the first faint awakenings of love, had she recognised it, reached him with the milk from his mother's torn and troubled body.

Next day I woke early as usual, before daylight. Kayleigh and Mark slept. I pulled aside the curtains and looked out at the unfamiliarity of the familiar scene below: the street luxuriating in moonlight, that strange brightness, not quite powerful enough to conquer the dark. Shadows fell differently, friendly shapes took on slightly sinister disguises; the moon showed the powerlessness of the pallid orange street lighting. Light shining in darkness: new life in my house ...

I revelled at what had happened over the last few months. My house, now a home once more, with the growing chaos of a new baby replacing the lifeless chaos of those wasted years. As I struggled to help Kayleigh care for Mark, I found I was beginning also to care for myself, slowly regaining my place in the human race. I started to say, 'Hello' to my neighbours, sheepishly at first; some were not the same neighbours as those in the days before the Tragedy, but they were still wary of me. We were progressing beyond, 'Lovely/dreadful day' to, 'How's your niece?'

As the weeks went by, Kayleigh became fascinated, obsessed almost, with the flow of milk passing daily from her to Mark. Its smell, which first disgusted her, became a delight. I marvelled at her patience, not something I would have expected from Kayleigh. She didn't seem to suffer from sleep deprivation, that torture of new parents.

'How did you sleep?' I would ask each morning.

'He slept OK between feeds. Mau, I'm hungry. I could murder bacon and eggs.'

I went to find the frying pan; it was nearly what I thought of as lunch time. Mark whimpered in Kayleigh's arms. She sat down instantly to feed him.

'He doesn't need to be fed every time he cries,' I said. 'Babies just whinge sometimes.' I was beginning to feel it was safe to offer advice.

'Why not feed him? He likes it, I'm not bothered.'

I watched the two of them through the kitchen door. What strange power had awakened in Kayleigh? The magic of motherhood. I began to have faith that, possibly, all could be well. Did I dare to hope? Hope for the future was emerging from all those past years of hopelessness. The idea of Mark being adopted was no longer discussed. The smell of burning bacon returned me to the present and I narrowly avoided another fire.

As I turned off the gas, tipped the flaming frying pan into the sink where it hissed violently, a cloud of steam rising to fill the kitchen, I remembered house insurance. Money had been leaving my account for years, but I never read the small print: what did it cover? I had no idea, and did not know where I put the literature. I must find it, and make sure it was adequate: no more risks. I took another rasher from the fridge and shut the kitchen door.

A health visitor came one morning; the hospital had suggested there might be Child Welfare concerns, perhaps a section 47 enquiry.

'Oh good,' she said to Kayleigh, brightly, 'you're feeding him.'

'He'd be dead if I weren't,' said Kayleigh.

'I meant he's still on the breast. That's excellent. Do you use a bottle at all?'

'What for? Lot of nuisance, washing up, and all. Besides me tits is best. Gives him a good start, see. He's less likely to catch things – know what I means? Germs and that. And he'll be brainier.'

I watched the health visitor listening to the lecture she must usually give herself.

'Kayleigh's breast feeding for England,' I said. The health visitor smiled. Why had the hospital been concerned?

Kayleigh was living only for Mark, bound to him by milk. Gradually she stopped complaining that he was a boy, learned to enjoy him. I watched her giving of herself. I remembered trying to 'establish a routine' which was supposed to give a child a sense of security, and the mother some control over her life. Kayleigh fitted herself round Mark's demands, and somehow a routine established itself, which suited all three of us. I would hear Mark wake any time between four and seven in the morning; Kayleigh instantly took him into her bed, fed him, and they both fell asleep together, waking at a respectable teenage early morning around eleven. I liked being alone in the mornings, there was less time for quarrelling with Kayleigh. Motherhood seemed so much easier than when I had done it.

This health visitor even coaxed Kayleigh to visit the unit where she could take Mark, and do her school work, get some GCSEs. When she complained that it was 'not for the likes of me', I told her that it was precisely for the likes of her. I said I had always dreamed of becoming a teacher. Now a long dead dream. Urged on by my stories of working in the library, she finally agreed to start in September, telling herself September was a long way off.

I thought the Krew were coming less often when they should have been at school. I heard the words GCSE and 'options' in their talk, without giggling. I could not remember much about the exams I had taken at school, except that I did well, could have gone to college. Memories of the boys' O levels came back: coaxing, bribing them with their favourite meals to revise; tantrums like two year olds; depression when they knew they had failed; deciding whether the dreadful sickness was nerves or appendicitis. Were the Krew going to go through all that? Their parents would probably not care how they did: would that make it easier?

Michael left school at sixteen, to take up his garage apprenticeship. John had done well at O levels, stayed on for the sixth form, but found himself a job in a bank before doing A levels. That had been a bitter disappointment to me. I spent hours berating his form teacher for letting him leave. The poor man had given up several of his lunch hours, trying to get John to change his mind. Would Kayleigh get a chance to make something of her life?

After Mark's arrival the Krew stopped asking to stay overnight. They were slightly in awe of this new Kayleigh, some of the old Kayleigh seemed to have been left behind in the hospital. Kayleigh and I started to give each other more space, nearly stopped trying to change each other, sensing that each was changing in different ways. Mark seemed to sleep longer than I remember either of my babies doing. I was sleeping longer, my gremlins were beginning to leave me in peace at night. Soon Kayleigh and I would be sharing breakfast.

With the warmer weather the girls started visiting the Tip again. How long would they continue to find strength in the magic of their island? Would it always be there when needed? Kayleigh said, 'Mark likes to see the trains.' She would carry him across the Tip in his sling. He was growing into a cheerfully alert baby. Almost every day one of the girls would bring a toy for him. Sam had picked up a 'baby gym' in the Salvation Army shop. I was glad that it looked a bit too big to hide under a coat, and had visions of babies climbing ropes and wall bars, which

I had so hated at school. I watched Mark trying to grasp the coloured objects floating out of reach above his head, laughing as he stretched, like some upturned crab struggling to right itself. Michael and John had been expected to sleep peacefully in their prams in the garden most of the day; none of the American talking toys, which I found so exasperating, existed in their babyhoods. One day Mark would realise that life was not all fun and flashing lights, but not yet.

* * *

It's much too hot in here, do they want us to burn to death? 'Old people can die of cold without even noticing.' What a wonderful way to go. The granite God reminds me of this advertisement which I saw in a paper, long ago, in the days when I still looked at papers, from some charity for the aged.

Where did I read, 'Young men shall see visions, old men shall dream dreams.' Or is it the other way round? I see no visions, have no dreams, except the vision of peace, the dream of nothingness. Of being one with all that is, for all is nothingness. All else is illusion. Does that make me Old? Here they see me as Old, I can hear it in their voices. I know I'm old, but not Old. That means wisdom. A wise woman. A witch?

Where do such ideas come from? From the Great Nothingness. The Great Oneness. For all is one. All is nothing. Nothing is. To be Old is to see this, and to understand it. All our striving, all our misery, all our joy, all is nothing. When we finally know this, we know that we, too, are nothing. All lost in the sea of nothingness.

The sea ... I would like to have seen the sea once more, before going. I think I would have a new relationship with it: not something to swim in, but to be marvelled at. The waves no longer to jump among, but listen to. Heeded ...

* * *

I remember that day on the beach with Kayleigh and Suzanne. I so wanted them to have what they had missed as children. But it was too late. Was that before Kay moved in with me? I'm not sure. Not sure of anything any more. Perhaps that was my farewell to the sea? I didn't realise it at the time, that late autumn day. The Indian summer seemed to have lasted for weeks. As October approached its end, it felt as if the sun would never admit defeat: even as the days shortened, the clocks went back, the hours of daylight were blue and sunny. The leaves clung tenaciously to the trees. Children would have to wait to scuffle through knee-high golden beech leaves, until the year was prepared to die. I needed to make up for all the years when I had let autumns pass me by; I revelled in it.

The seaside, I thought, we'll go to the seaside. Just the thing, get Kayleigh out, give her some fresh air and exercise. There would be no crowds at this time of year. It was so beautifully warm. If this had been August it would have been unbearably hot. Now the heat was a delight, and the risk of sunburn slight as the sun sank lower each day.

'What for?' said Kayleigh again. Her lack of enthusiasm infuriated me; I'd fondly assumed she would be delighted at the prospect, even more as she said she'd never been to the seaside, except on a school trip when she was in the juniors. 'I've done without the sea for fifteen years. I thinks I can go a bit longer. Wait till the baby's old enough, like.'

I tried to hide my disappointment. I had dreamed of sharing so many delights with Kayleigh; I forgot that when she saw the sea she would probably say something like, 'OK. So?' Or, perhaps, if she was really impressed, she might condescend to say, 'Cool.'

I treasured my memories of early seaside holidays with Mother and Father. Now I wanted to seize Kayleigh by the scruff of her neck, make her experience the wonder that was the sea. After much argument, Kayleigh finally agreed, on condition that Suze could come too. Miraculously Suze's parents agreed, and paid her train fare.

The train ran swiftly along its allotted track. All three of us savoured the novelty of being inside a train looking out this time. I had not been on a train for so long that I had no idea what they were like inside now. Outside they were brash, proud, shameless, hurrying towards the future. Smaller older trains, some decorated with advertisements, hurrying more slowly, were cheerfully self-important. I could remember 'corridor trains', where two rows of passengers sat facing each other, a door leading to a corridor. Local trains had no corridors, no escape from your neighbour. There was always that frisson of fear, although the next station was never far away.

We watched the lines running straight beside us, then veering away, as another line suddenly appeared from nowhere. Sometimes we joined this line, and swayed sideways with it, more often rusting useless rails ran alongside us for miles. We passed blackened red brick railway buildings, clinging on, like our Shack, to a past that refused to disappear. We changed in Bristol, that triumphant Victorian splendour of a station, built when steam was transforming the world. Its golden stone shone in the sun, illuminating the glory of the bygone age, when travel meant soot in the eyes, billows of smoke, hiss of steam, tips for porters, cardboard tickets filled in with fountain pens, excitement, adventure, even in a few hours' journey to the sea. The dirty train whispered of another world.

The girls soon tired of the novelty of travel, and started a game, imagining who their fellow passengers might be, giggling loudly. I was embarrassed. I tried to pretend they were nothing to do with me, reliving the last time I had been to the seaside, shortly after Husband left …

I had gone to this coast, telling myself I might find some peace, some hope in the sea, perhaps wash myself in the Great Green Deep. I had always found strength in the sea. When I got there that day I couldn't even put on my swimming costume. Instead, I walked along the cliff path for miles. I reached another tiny seaside village and saw three telephones in a row, none of them standard BT: two could only be used to ring 999, the other was for the Samaritans. None had looked as if they could work. I shivered. Was that why I had come? For the truly lasting peace? I shivered again, saw a bus timetable; I could return by bus just in time for the last train.

That long walk came back to me so clearly: it had been February, with a February menacing sky, a grey winter sea. Light rain stopped for a while, as grey shades moved across the sky. Who would have thought there could be so many shades of grey, from near black, to dirty white? Grey sky, grey clouds, grey sea, confronted me. So easy to slip into their clutches. The changelessly changing sea, was always there, its tides obeying the moon's mysterious powers, eroding the cliffs, which tumbled at its command, revealing tidy strata, like drawers in the filing cabinet in a well organised office: the secrets of the origins of the earth filed away for those who care to read. Then a landslip: the horizontal rows were now almost vertical. The message slewed sideways, yet was still readable.

The grandeur of the grey said that nothing was reliable, everything transient, made of dreams. I absently picked up a fossil, a pebble, rounded by the sea, smooth to the touch, history in my hand. This delicate pattern of twigs and leaves set in the harshness of stone was once a living, growing plant.

This inaccessible stretch of coast was so far untainted by the rampage of holiday makers. Here were no promenades, piers, lewd laughter, cafés in the sand: only the sea. Did we build our holiday resorts at the seaside to bring the infinite down to our level? Why was the holy sea essential to even a bawdy, drunken holiday?

Those telephones: did people choose to end their lives by coming to the sea? Or did they decide to end their tidy lives, when the sea showed them just how insignificant they were? How many had been saved by those possibly useless telephones? On that far off day I caught the bus, caught the train, returned to my loneliness, my hopelessness. Did the Samaritans keep me alive then, or was it cowardice? I remembered long hours of weeping into the telephone, which was then silent for years until Kayleigh came …

We got out of the train at the little village, no longer home to a Holiday Camp, unsure now of its identity, particularly in October. Both girls would have enjoyed the holiday camp more than the beach, and were disappointed that the garish 'Pleasure Park' was padlocked. An air of discreet decay hung over the place. A boarded up ice-cream kiosk was for sale. The pink cliff, with layers of green and grey rock, was falling into the sea. The lighthouse no longer needed its keeper. Yachts joined in the busy fishing boats' clunking music in the marina, mingled with the lapping of the waves and the seagulls' screams. Yet the sea spray still tasted of tears, the ancient chapel still kept watch from the hill, history quietly fading.

Kayleigh, now obviously pregnant, had to be persuaded to go down all those steps to the beach, and once there needed to go all the way up again for the loo. She grumbled, but came back.

'Exercise is good for Baby,' I said, thinking I sounded like a midwife.

'Perhaps. But what about me? Not much use to Baby if I goes and collapses from all them fucking steps.'

'I'm going for a swim.'

Both girls stared at me. Neither of them had thought of swimming in late October, or at any time in that murky water. Probably not at all.

'It should still be warm, after all that sun,' I said, wriggling into my faded costume, which sagged around my slight body. I watched their embarrassment with amusement.

'Shall we hold the towel up round you?' asked Suze.

'No bother. I'm old enough not to care. If some dirty old man wants to watch me, that's his problem.'

Kayleigh could not resist snatching a quick peep at me as I bent down to pull up my costume, my breasts hanging like the empty udders of an over-milked cow, grey, with blue lines. Loose flesh hung from where my stomach should be, like a turkey's neck. I skipped down to the sea like a child, and splashed into the waves, ignoring the accumulated debris of plastic bottles, half decayed shoes, picnic boxes and dead bladderwort.

As I slowly swam out, my enjoyment increasing with every stroke, Kayleigh and Suze wandered down the sand to the water's edge, took off their shoes, rolled up their jeans, and paddled. Something of my enthusiasm must have reached them as the surprisingly warm water washed over their toes and waves splashed them. Neither would admit that they envied me, as each secretly savoured the power of the sea. An unexpectedly large wave caught them, their giggles were muted, as they wandered back up the beach, jeans clinging to wet legs.

Their voices carried out to me over the water, where I was bobbing about on the waves, like a seagull.

'Maude's gross. She's got no hair round her fanny: what a place to go bald. What if she can't get back, Suze?'

'Course she can.'

'She said as she hadn't been swimming for years. She's fucking far out.'

'Forget it. Look, she's turned round.'

They watched as I swam parallel to the shore for a while, then turned back. Were they aware of something out of balance: they should have been swimming, enjoying the water on their bare flesh, me relaxing and keeping a careful eye on them. Not the other way round.

I'd almost forgotten the girls. I'd swum out further than I intended as the salt water on my skin brought back the joy of sea bathing. Now I turned, I was beginning to tire. I looked at the little town, still called an Island, although the Victorians had built a causeway, linking it to the mainland. Sometimes a flood tide covered the causeway, reminding everyone that it was still essentially an island, at the mercy of the sea's treacherous tides and hostile weather. Unique, like all islands, yet it shared the essential island personality, linked to all other islands far beneath the sea. I let the gentle salt water hold me in its cleansing embrace, turning to see, far out, the two tiny nature reserve islands where the gulls rule ferociously. They reminded me of how Shellie once ran screaming over the Tip, sure gulls were chasing her. The girls threw stones at them and they flew away, feigning indifference. I turned over on to my back, and floated, letting the gentle waves lift me and then let me down again.

Kayleigh and Suze, watching, worried again that I was floating because I was exhausted; could not go on. But my mind was drifting to fictional islands: desert islands, treasure islands, where the inhabitants and their authors, wove paradises of possibilities, happy endings. Holy islands. Only *The Lord of the Flies* offered a more sinister picture, and this was the boys, not the island. So different from the Krew's island Tip.

Tired now, I turned towards the shore, glad of the help of the incoming tide. Had it been outgoing it might have dragged me out with it. I was not as strong as I once was, and the sea was as powerful as ever. No one can defeat the sea; behind its rejuvenating power lies savage destruction.

Before my eyes could focus on the few people on the beach,

I recognised Kayleigh, half exulting in her obvious pregnancy, half ashamed of it.

I swam to the shore and walked back to the girls, splashing water over myself and them as they ran to meet me, and then ran away squealing like the children they were.

'Mind us, Mau.' I laughed with them. Not chiding them for not joining me, as I had always done with the boys.

'I needs a pee again,' said Kayleigh. 'It's that baby.'

I set off up the beach at a pace they had to hurry to keep up with. Kayleigh puffed up after me, holding her warm, soft bulge. She shivered as if she had been in the sea.

It was nearly time to go home. The sun was sinking slowly; the sky first took on a sea green tinge, then, as the sea darkened, the sky shone triumphant in every shade of red and gold.

'I have shone today. I have lived and given life,' said the sun, setting the sky on fire.

I watched, trembling at my unlived life. I prayed, perhaps to the sun, for Kayleigh and her baby. The wonder of the sunset momentarily penetrated the girls' giggles. To me it was a sign, an assurance, of continuity in the face of perpetual transience. Everything passes, everything is. The sunset reassures us that the sun will rise again. We will not rise again, but become part of an eternal sunset. We all watched the darkness take control, moving through all the shades of blue, from azure to blackberry, before colour disappeared completely into the dark, as the train hurried us home ...

The sea has been a large part of my life, even though I've always lived so far from it. I no longer need to swim in it to know that I'm part of it. Perhaps I should have gone to the sea, not the Moor, to make an end. But there would have been too many coastguards, and I know that I shall finally be one with the sea, when I am nothing. When I am at peace.

* * *

'Visitors for you, Maude.'

I look up. There they are: Kay, looking angry, almost the old Kayleigh. But it is an anger mingled with love. A look of loving anger, the two mingling into an expression I cannot read.

Mark skips along beside Kay, looking really smart: perhaps he was sick on the way here, and has just been changed. He charges across the ward as if he knew it, then back to Kay saying, 'Where do they keep the train sets here?'

He loves his pre-school. I would have liked to see him grow up, at least a little. Have taught him to read.

Where have all the years gone? The years since he was born. All mingled and mixed up in my mind. Years of nothing much happening, but everything happening. Life going on. Just an ordinary, extraordinary life. We all grew and changed. I'll always be grateful for that.

Kay and Sue: their own people. They have their own values, not mine. How much must I tell them? I've never lied to Kay, but I've not always told her all the truth. Must she know of my death sentence now? The truth will come out at death, but until then, surely I can keep some of my secret? What is truth anyway?

Sue is here too, and her latest young man. Perhaps he drove them here?

I show Mark the button to press to raise or lower the bed, and this keeps him occupied until a nurse tells him to stop.

Kay, or is it Kayleigh, says angrily, 'Maude, how could you? I thought I knew you, but I never for a moment believed you could do this to me ...'

I don't listen to it all.

'... Of course I guessed you must be ill. All that falling over, forgetting things. But I thought you'd tell me in your own good time. That would be like you, to tell me when it was obvious to anyone with eyes. But I waited for your time ...'

Was it really so obvious?

'But to try and leave us without saying goodbye, without me being able to say thank you. No explanation. Romantic, perhaps, but not like you, Maude.'

She pauses for breath, comes down on top of me and kisses me on the lips. We've seldom kissed. We started hugging when Mark was born, and occasionally she puts a dry kiss on my cheek. But full mouth kissing has not been our way. This kiss is almost sexual. I haven't been kissed like this for over half a century. I start to cry.

Mark climbs up on to Kay's lap, and peers down at me. 'Why is Aunty Maude in bed?'

I can only smile.

'She's been very ill, Mark. The hospital are making her better.' Kay strokes his cheek.

I shake my head. If only. She strokes my cheek.

Now I understand just what it was that we shared on the Tip. A sense of oneness. Of belonging, of caring, of all being part of some greater whole. Somehow, just by being there for each other, the Krew managed to cope with problems that no child should be called upon to endure. The Tip was somewhere to hang out and have a moan. But it was also a magic island. Will they be able to create magic islands throughout their lives? Perhaps the real magic was within each one of them? Each one an island, and like islands, each, in some mysterious way, linked deep beneath the oceans. These links must surely survive.

'Maude,' says Kay. 'Maude, don't cry. I'm only angry because I love you.'

What is Love? It's not the same as Worry or Grief at loss. I think I mistook these for Love in the past. It's more than, but simpler than them. Is it just being there?

I don't want to die here in hospital.

My head is suddenly filled with the voice of a boy soprano singing sweetly, 'Lord now lettest thou thy servant depart in peace ...' So beautiful.

* * *

I hadn't remembered it was this steep. Mustn't fall yet. This was going to be harder than I thought. And colder … I was not getting any younger … Stop it Maude. Don't even think in clichés. At least I was not going to get any older … I was not afraid. Was that true? Why should I be afraid? Soon I would merge with this holy granite, losing myself, becoming part of all that is. Myself at last.

I sat, leaning against a long fallen log, emerald green with moss. In front was a dying tree, whose misshapen trunk and stunted, twisted branches, clung to life: its death throes creating a weird sculpture. I sat. I could feel the past all around me. The past spoke to me, even if I could not be sure what it was saying

Why did they erect those stones? They must have had a reason. Perhaps, in their search for the meaning of their existence, they thought their God lived below the Moor. Perhaps they saw the tors as God breaking through from below to join them. Did they erect stones to complement the natural, the divine, tors? God, perhaps, was in that granite. Somehow, as I sat among the tors and the granite, I felt, really felt, part of the past. I was being absorbed by it. In time I would become part of the future, to anyone who could understand this. Perhaps Kay. Certainly not Kayleigh.

Ancient granite, fossils, so old we can't comprehend. Lives that have touched my own, but without my knowing, so briefly.

I was ready now to be part of the day. I would live in death far more than I ever did in life. My life returned to me, not to taunt me with the wasted years, but to remind me of love, of good times. There were good times, when I was a mother, and when I was with Kayleigh, Suze and the others, and darling little Mark. No one would believe this story if I told it. Yet the strangest things are true if we allow them to be. It is untruth that is so frighteningly credible.

Useless to regret the might-have-beens, the if-onlys. These have made me who I am. Whether Michael and I will meet again no longer matters. I am ready to move on, to be more truly me, as I submit myself to the eternal, to become part of the infinite We.

Was this the West? The clouds sailing ahead were pink. I looked round, yes, behind me the sky was gold, gleaming like satin, a colour to die for. The pink streaking the West was mere reflection. Soon it would be impossible to look East: it would be as blinding as the West at sunset. A few minutes ago I had been climbing this great Moor, the sun rising with me. When I had gone down to this valley, the sun had seemed to set. Now, even here, He had risen. No longer the milky, misty sun more like the moon, but a full and glaring sun shone on the strange pastel green of the grass beneath the frosty dew. The sun would be most powerful when it came from the South: the magic, invisible light, seen only in darkness, comes from the North. I would travel North.

Sunrise, sunset: the beginning and the end of a day, or a life. So similar, so simple. The days were short, only a few hours separated the rising and setting of the sun. The bracken and heather had put on their warm winter reds and browns. A good time to join the darkness, and come to the light. Suddenly another mist blew over the Moor, hiding my view. How wet it was, how satisfyingly cold.

I used to wonder if I would still enjoy walking if I lost my sight. Now, engulfed in mist, I knew I would. Soon I would lose more than my sight, but knew that, in some form, I'd continue to walk this granite for ever. The wind picked up. The view returned. A pity about the degree. It was not too late: it's never too late. I was loving studying, sharing ideas, so different from sharing with the Krew. All that was over now.

I would not be escaping, but moving on. Once I was afraid, I clung to the past, pulled Grief's dank cloak more tightly around me, as this narrow valley held on to the gloom of night, when beyond, all proclaimed the arrival of a new day. Fear of death, I realised, is the price we pay for our belief in individuality. We can only be free by being one with life itself. I choose this freely.

It is time. This is not a denial of life, but an affirmation. It is time. I sit facing West. It is Sunday morning quiet up here, too early in the year for the dawn chorus: I am almost sad that I will never hear that again in the flesh. Silence reigns: the silent singing of the stars. The silence of death. The peace of death. The silence of stone, of sand, of solitude.

A solitary barn owl hoots in the distance. The day is coming surreptitiously: the darkness fades, and the fragile tracery of the trees' dark branches comes into focus; their tops, like tangling spiders' webs, sway to and fro, crossing and re-crossing each other, and disappear into the sky. The treetops' fan-like shapes, waving in all directions, suggest infinite possibilities. This unfolding panorama can only be seen in winter, through these tangled, bare branches. Is that the red danger flag drooping sadly, away on the Moor's far horizon? Colour emerges in the sky: deep blue, tinged with turquoise. I see small patches of snow clinging to sunless corners. The trees' shapes become more definite, finer. The moon fades, the sky lightens, the darkness becomes streaked with pink clouds. Soon even the tiniest twig is clear against the fast lightening sky, each one linked, by circuitous routes, to the tree's roots, the source of their life. The grandeur of the Moor is appearing all around me. I will worship the God of the granite, I am ready …

Gracious Granite God, be with me. Support Kay in the days and years to come. Let Mark know true love as he grows. Make yourself known to them. I am coming to you. Bless me, Mother.

The music has gone. Birdsong has mingled with the mysterious crackling of the Moor. I feel less cold now. Could this be it? Is that a dog? Oh no. Voices …

* * *

I can hear Kay calling to me, 'Maude, Maude, love. Don't go. Stay with us. Let me look after you … Nurse! Quick.'

But I want to go.

Scrambling. Voices. More voices. Wheels. Hurry. They want to make me live again. Beneath it all, do I sense that perfect peace?

Do I hear Kay, saying quietly, but with great authority, 'Let her go.' Or is that just what I want to hear?

The End

About the Author

Mary Brown is the author of three non-fiction books; two about prison. Her long career in adult education included teaching in an open prison and tutoring for the Open University, after which she became a Quaker Prison Chaplain. She has also seen prison from the other side of the bars, spending ten days in HM Prison Holloway in 1960 following a peace protest. Much of Mary's writing is about those on the margins of society.

A Quaker, mother of four children and grandmother of eight, Mary now enjoys retirement in the beautiful Cotswold countryside. Written after her retirement and published in her 80s, *I Used to Be* is Mary's first novel.

Edward Douglas Miller founded Remarkable Eco Solutions in 1996 inspired by a passion for the environment. His first product took used plastic cups and turned them into pencils. He said, 'We didn't just say the pencils were recycled, we also said this pencil was made from a plastic cup, so people could engage with the story.'

Ed Miller's mission became to educate Britain to be more environmentally responsible, and he invented recycled, innovative products that for many years were sold in Britain's high street stores, including Oxfam. He was behind the 'I Used to Be...' slogan that appeared on his products in such forms as 'I used to be... a juice carton' or 'I used to be... a car tyre' or in the case of the slogan that caught Maude's eye on the front of what turned out to be an empty notebook: 'I used to be... a cardboard box'.

Remarkable Eco Solutions was dissolved in 2016.

If you have enjoyed this book, please consider leaving a review for Mary to let her know what you thought of her work.

You can find out more about Mary on her author page on the Fantastic Books Store. While you're there, why not browse our delightful tales and wonderfully woven prose?

www.fantasticbooksstore.com

Made in the USA
Columbia, SC
07 December 2017